Her Saltwater Cowboy

JULIE CAROBINI

DOLPHIN GATE BOOKS

Chapter One

His father couldn't be serious.

Chance Sutter ran his hand across the scruff of his face as he listened to unexpected news. Earlier this morning, he had debated whether to bother with the razor, but after a lousy night's sleep, the scruff won out. He figured his father wouldn't even notice him over in the barn with a day's growth on his skin. Or in the horse stalls. Or even when he wandered into the farmhouse kitchen for a late breakfast after he'd finished his early morning chores.

And he especially hadn't expected to run into him in the dining room, long after the ranch owner and the hands usually ate their morning meal.

Ace Sutter, Chance's father, hated it when he and his brothers showed up at the ranch without a shave. A holdover from when they were teens, and their mother would line them up and shave every last pubescent whisker from their mugs before church.

She had been gone for years now, and his two brothers had rarely been to visit, but their father kept up the tradition.

Apparently, that's where his father's love of tradition ended.

"Look me in the eye, son." Ace no longer towered over Chance, of course, but his mountainous presence was felt just the same, even as they sat at his mother's favorite scarred-up wooden table waiting for a hearty, but simple meal. "Rafael and his bride will be moving in soon, and I want them to feel welcome."

These were the last words he had expected to hear this morning. Even a scolding about his whiskers would have been more welcome than this.

Chance lifted his chin as Willow, their new cook, breezed through the dining room and laid plates piled high with eggs, bacon, sausage, and a perfunctory slice of orange in front of them. Willow looked unflustered by the sudden change in her new employer's eating schedule.

On any other day, Chance would have wandered inside mid-morning, taken a plate of food for himself after the ranch hands had eaten, and gobbled it up quickly and quietly before heading back to work. Usually, the aroma made his stomach grumble in a good way, rather than lurch, as it was doing now. He avoided Willow's eyes as she bustled right back out of the room.

After she'd gone, Chance speared his father with a look. "How long have you planned this … transition?"

Ace stared back at his son. He reached for the salt, turned the shaker over, and generously seasoned his breakfast. He took a bite and chewed it slowly, offering Chance a pensive expression, the kind that caused a dip in his brow.

Chance sat back, waiting. His father put down his fork. "You don't worry about that. What I want from you is to make sure your cousin has all his questions answered about our operations here. He'll be relying on you. As will Bella, his wife."

"Me?"

"You're the only son who's stayed around long enough to know something about this place."

He ignored the tinge of bitterness in his father's tone because, honestly, what he said was only partially true. Yes, Chance's brothers had left the state, returning for funerals—like their mother's—and holidays, when possible. But all three of them had grown up on the ranch, knew the ins and outs, what needed doing, and when.

Only he had decided to eventually return to make his life here at Sutter Creek Ranch in the shadow of the Topatopa Mountains. He figured he would step in and resume daily duties, and, when the time was right, take on more. Then it happened. Sparky, their longtime foreman, retired.

And Chance was ready to step into those boots.

Only, instead of handing the foreman position to the man who'd ridden out every storm on this ranch, Ace had given it to someone who hadn't stepped onto the property in years.

Chance kept his voice even. "You might've talked to me first."

Ace gave a dry chuckle. "Didn't realize I needed your permission."

Chance ignored the dig. "If you'd asked, you would have heard I was ready to take on more. That I've *been* ready."

Ace gave him a long, unreadable look.

"I've hauled fence posts, kept the inventory clean, coordinated the vet visits, trained the new hires ..."

"Ran off to the beach," Ace interjected.

Chance paused, keeping his voice level. "I've been here every necessary minute. Day in, day out."

Ace took a sip of coffee from his mug. "But for how long?"

"I'm not leaving." Chance leaned his arms on the table. "Besides, the ranch could use an audit before we go hiring anybody."

"You let me worry about the ranch's funds. I don't need some fancy degree to show me what's in black and white."

Chance held his tongue at his father's dig about his education, but was not about to let up. "What about the old barn roof we've been talking about replacing, and the cattle gates that need replacing?"

"The barn roof'll hold for now, and Rafael can handle the gates once he's caught up with the other changes around here."

Chance's jaw clicked. "The barn roof definitely won't hold out much longer ..." he muttered.

He took a breath and forced himself to sit back and absorb what he'd just learned. Finally, he said, "I've been right here, all along, Ace, carrying my weight—carrying the weight of three hands at times."

Ace paused, his focus on his son. "It's true you've done well. I've been impressed with your work, though I thought you might have left us again by now."

"Never said I had plans to leave."

His father's eyes blazed. "You've never said you had plans to stay either."

Quiet enveloped them for a beat. He didn't need this. If Chance wanted to, he could swap his boots for dress shoes and go back to corporate America. Muscles in his gut clenched. "And Rafael? You're sure he won't leave again?"

Ace looked away. "You don't know anything about that."

Chance shifted, but he did not back down. "I know your

fight with him years ago made our mother cry. He was like a little brother to us, and then, suddenly, he wasn't." His mother had called him with the story of how his teenage cousin showed up drunk and ornery in the middle of the night to have it out with his uncle. Ace had thrown the kid off the property that night, and Rafael swore he would never return. He had made good on his word. Until recently.

"That boy came back here and made his peace. Asked me for forgiveness. He's my sister's son." On the word "sister," Ace's voice cracked, and Chance knew his father had regrets about not reaching out to his kin before her death. "It took a lot of humility for him to come here and face me again."

"So that's it. He and his family are moving to the ranch, and I don't have a say in the matter."

"You don't need one."

Willow peeked in through the doorway. "Would either of you like seconds?"

Ace dusted his hands in front of himself and pushed away from the table. "No, ma'am. You've overfed me as it is."

Willow smiled as she walked over and whisked Ace's empty plate from the table. "I'm glad to hear it." She glanced at Chance's plate and frowned. "Was something wrong with your food, Chance?"

Ace stood. "My son's not all that pleased with the company right now."

Chance rose to his feet. He unlocked his jaw. "Not exactly true."

"Oh no? Then prove it by helping me ready this place for our new residents." Ace swung a look at the cook. "And I'll need your help as well, Willow."

"Yes, of course, Ace. Absolutely. Anything you need."

"The wife of our new foreman is a vegetarian, by the way."

Chance tried not to laugh outright at the slight lift of Willow's delicate eyebrows. "Not a problem," she sang out as she carried both plates from the dining room and into the kitchen.

Ace turned to leave, then pivoted back. He reached over and placed a meaty hand on his son's shoulder. "I'm trusting in you."

Those words carried weight like gold. A million memories clipped through Chance's head, like slides in one of those old projectors. It's why he had come back after college and, later, a corporate accounting job took him away.

It was also the lack of hearing such sentiments that kept him and his brothers away for so long. He'd hoped to change that, to smooth things over between his father and brothers, so they could be the family they had once been. Maybe even lure them back to the ranch someday.

But how would he convince them now when their father all but gave the running of the place over to their cousin, who had broken from the family so many years ago?

Chance gave his father a sober look, but nodded once quickly, hoping to placate him. He had a horse to ride, fencing to fix, parts to order. Honestly, he'd rather be mucking out stalls than be in this stifling dining room a minute longer, turning over dark thoughts in his head.

His father turned to leave and stopped, eyeing him. "And son?"

"Yes?"

"Make sure to shave before dinnertime."

Willow slid the last of her homemade chicken pot pies into the oven, set the timer, then stepped back. It was late afternoon, and the familiar aroma would be filling the enormous kitchen soon. Part of her couldn't wait, while the other dreaded it because that smell carried with it memories that would never be again.

She let out a sigh and looped a stray tendril of hair over her ear. No sense brooding over the past. Or worse, divulging to anyone here that she'd made this move to be closer to her mother, something she could not have done without this job. Most of their past had been sold, and the more she learned to move forward, the better off she would be.

Thankfully, she had her mama's recipes to keep her company through the long, hard days of running a kitchen for hungry ranchers. Hard work and honesty had been knitted into the fabric of who she was, so a thread of guilt always seemed to work its way loose whenever she found herself thinking too long about this position she had accepted.

Willow found her way to the far end of the meandering, scarred kitchen island, the one topped with wood gouged by years' worth of meals. She poured herself a glass of lemonade from the pitcher on the island and drank it down, letting the coolness of it refresh her while waiting for dinner to cook.

She glanced around, taking it all in. By all accounts, Patsy, her predecessor, had run this place without error. The woman had been friendly by nature, yet tough when she needed to be. And her food was above reproach. Not to mention … complicated. More than once, Willow's eyes had tired from taking in the long lists of ingredients that Patsy filled the pantry with and often rolled into her dishes as deftly as she might have pulled on a sock.

When Willow had heard about this position up here in Topa Springs, right near where she needed to be, she believed she'd been given a gift from God himself. He had made a way for her amid a trial she couldn't fathom.

And yet, had she been completely honest when she had accepted the position as cook, knowing well that her cooking skills had been tested mainly on only her mother and herself?

A door from the outside opened, slamming against a wall, followed by the heavy sound of boots landing on freshly washed and dried tile floors. Chance marched into the room and tossed his hat onto the island. He opened the fridge with such force that the condiments on the door rattled, and he hauled out a head of lettuce, sliced cheddar, roast beef, mustard, and a gallon of milk. He spun toward the cabinets, yanked open a silverware drawer, and tossed out a butter knife, letting it bounce across the wooden surface. From an upper cabinet, he retrieved a plate and a mug, then slammed the door shut.

Willow winced at that show of hostility, hoping the intricately etched glass inlaid in that cabinet door had not just gained a fracture. She watched as he proceeded to make himself the most haphazard, asymmetrical sandwich she'd ever seen. He gobbled it down after that, still unaware that he had an audience.

It might've stayed that way if he hadn't slammed down his mug after gulping back his milk in one long swig.

Willow cleared her throat.

Chance stopped cold when he spotted her sitting there,

his hand still wrapped around that empty mug. Was that a milk mustache?

When she saw the fury in his dark eyes, she chose to keep that question to herself. And a small part of her had a mind to apologize for taking a break at all. The other part of her remembered her mother's voice in her head, admonishing her to stand up for herself.

Even if, in this case, that meant staying seated.

He nodded once. "Willow."

"Chance."

"You been there the whole time?"

"I have."

He pressed his lips together and nodded. Then picked up his dishes and dumped the whole mess into the sink with a clatter.

Willow reached him in a few quick steps, placing herself between Chance and the sink. She leaned her backside against the counter and crossed her arms.

He furrowed his brow, confusion in his eyes. "You mad about something?"

"I'd appreciate it if you would be more careful with the dishes."

He appeared to shrug off her statement, a cocky half-grin rising on his face.

Willow stiffened, pulling her crossed arms more tightly around her. She sucked in a breath. "Listen, you coming in here banging drawers and throwing food around like a hungry beast less than an hour before supper is—is, well, it's a little insulting."

"That right?" He groaned like an angry child and ran a hand through his full head of burnished brown hair. His face still wore the scruff from this morning, only now it had turned thicker, darker. If he were going to shave it off in time for dinner, he'd better get a move on.

Unless he had decided to defy Ace's request?

Willow bit the inside of her lip. Growing up the only daughter of a single mother had not prepared her for the insolence of men, especially directed toward each other. How had Patsy handled their sparring? By ignoring it or by chasing them out of the kitchen with a broom?

She laughed.

Chance shrank back. "What's so funny?"

Willow shook her head. "Please. No. Just …" She was about to tell him she'd take care of his mess this time. After all, that was her job—to feed the men and care for the kitchen. But she sobered quickly. Ace had made it clear from day one of her job here that she had very large and well-worn shoes to fill.

This room is your domain, Willow, and I expect you to manage it as such.

She glanced again at Chance, licked her lips, and said, "The dishwasher's dirty."

"Meaning?"

She pointed toward the sink. "Meaning it's just waitin' for *more* dirty dishes. Yours."

His eyes expanded briefly, light from the afternoon sun illuminating their indescribable color, followed by a flash of … annoyance? Then a small, closed-mouth smile spread across Chance's face. "So you're giving me my come-uppance."

"I wouldn't be as dramatic as all that."

He leaned a hand on the counter, considering her. "You're serious."

"As a heart attack."

He nodded, pressing those lips together harder still, a bob to his head as he weighed the situation. She tried not to stare at the way his mouth curved as he thought, nor think about the fact that she'd had to pull her gaze away from him more than once since moving up here. Learning and organizing filled her head—that and how she would ever find time during the week to visit her mother. No room for anything … frivolous.

"Well, then, I suppose I ought to follow orders." He stepped close enough to her that she could smell the earth on him. He slid his gaze down her face, and her breath hitched. His voice carried low. "May I?"

Willow's mouth went dry.

He cocked a brow. Then he smiled that crooked grin at her.

Oh. Quickly, she moved away from the sink to give him access. From the corners of her gaze, she watched as Chance dug his used dishes and silverware out of the sink, quietly opened the dishwasher door, and gently found a place for each.

Without a word, he closed the dishwasher, straightened, and trained that knee-melting gaze on her. "Anything else, ma'am?"

Was he contrite? Or trying to intimidate her? Discernment hadn't always been one of her strong points, though she was trying to overcome it now by questioning everything.

"Yes," she said finally, gaining steam. "Go on and shave before dinner."

Chance threw his head back at this, the first laugh she'd seen from the man all day. "Yes, ma'am." Then he grabbed his hat, stuck it back on his head, and marched right back out the kitchen door.

Chapter Two

Days later, Willow stepped out of church, the late morning sun kissing her cheeks. Ace had made it clear that Sunday mornings were hers alone, and for that she'd been grateful.

Another reason to be grateful: a spirit renewed. The pastor's sermon had centered her somehow, reminding Willow that she was not alone in this life, though it felt like it a lot of the time.

But Jesus had not come to earth to live and die and rise again only for his story to be shelved like so many books from the past. He was to be known and his sacrifices to be remembered for the life he continued to give all those who believed.

She hung onto that truth with everything she had and found herself lingering on her thoughts when a familiar deep voice called out to her.

"Good morning, Willow."

Ace rambled out the side door of the old church and raised a hand in her direction.

She slowed. "Hello, Ace."

He wiped his forehead with a hanky and stuffed it into his back pocket, drawing a slow breath. "I don't usually use this time to talk business, but I'm glad I caught you. Our new foreman, Rafael—you met him some weeks back—will be moving up to the ranch this week. He'll be bringing his wife, Bella, with him, and they'll be staying in Sparky's old place."

Willow gasped, but quickly covered her mouth with her fingers. From what she'd been told, Sparky had helped Ace run this place for decades, and that cabin hadn't seen an update since. She didn't dare imagine the shape it was in.

Ace laughed heartily at her knee-jerk reaction. "Don't you worry about that old cabin. Some of the hands will be fixing things there this week in time for the couple to arrive. Kit, being the housekeeper, will tidy it all up."

"I-I'm sorry if I was—"

"That obvious?" He winked. "You were, but I understand. We want it to become their own, of course, but we will be handing it over in good shape first."

"That sounds lovely."

"And this is where you come in, Willow. I'd like you to plan a welcome party for Rafael and Bella for this Friday evening, and I want it to be done up right."

"Absolutely." Her mind raced, hoping she had both the street sense and the skills to cook foods fancier than pot pies and hearty meats, though maybe those would be enough. "About how many should I plan for?"

He puckered his mouth and looked up toward the heavens. "I'd say close to sixty."

She swallowed. Maybe if she waited long enough, if she didn't respond, he would correct himself. *Oh, hahaha, excuse my mental fart, darlin'! I meant ten people, not sixty!*

Instead, Ace added, "Give or take a handful."

"So … we'll be … gathering …"

"In the barn. Yes. I'll have the hands pull tables out of storage and set 'em up. You can come up with some kind of frou-frou for them, I take it?"

Feed sixty-plus people. Put frou-frou on at least eight tables, maybe ten. Sure-sure-sure. "Of course." She put on a smile. "I'll see what blooms are available in the garden and create some arrangements for the tables."

"Wonderful." He turned to go but stopped and snapped his fingers. "Recruit Chance to help you. Don't let him give you any guff. I want to see him doing some of the heavy lifting. Understood?"

"Yes, sir."

Ace grinned. "I will see you at suppertime. Enjoy your morning."

A half hour later, as she sat with her feet soaking in the creek down on the south end of the ranch, she fretted. Why hadn't she asked Ace for a menu? For suggestions? For a list of foods Patsy might have served?

Because … she was afraid. If she asked those questions, it would make it seem like she wasn't up for this task. She glanced at her phone and wrinkled her nose. In addition to Sunday mornings being for church, she'd also decided to spend as much time outdoors as possible. It stirred up her creativity, and, for a few brief hours, helped her think about something other than her worries.

Except today. Ace's request had all but upended her peaceful morning.

"Hello, Sarge."

Willow jerked a look up. Chance stood nearby, his face solemn, his hat tipped down.

"Chance?"

"Got any new orders for me today?"

Ah. He was still annoyed with her for asking him to clean up after himself. She quirked a smile at him, one to match the cocky expression he wore. "As a matter of fact, I do."

He stepped closer, his boots cracking a twig. "Let me guess. You want me to start washing my dishes in the creek."

"No."

"Doing the laundry out here on an old washboard."

"Negative."

He squatted down, his face level with hers, those kaleidoscope eyes trained on her. He gave off notes of tobacco and vanilla. "Then what is it, Miss Willow, that you'd like me to do today?"

She turned her head to focus on the creek, licking her lips to chase away her sudden dry mouth. "It's not today that I need your help, Chance. But soon."

"Oh?"

She glanced at him over her shoulder. "Your father has asked me to throw a large party for the new foreman and his wife. It's … this coming Friday night."

An edge to Chance's jaw appeared. He stood abruptly and kicked the dust from his boots.

Willow turned all the way around now. "You okay?"

He stared at her for a beat, tipped his head, and touched his hat lightly before stepping backward. "Goodbye."

"Wait a second. Chance? You haven't given me your answer about Friday."

"No."

"No, as in, you did give me your answer? Or … Chance, are you telling me you won't help me?"

He smiled now, that cockiness showing up out of nowhere. "Bingo."

Willow narrowed her eyes. "That's not actually an option."

"Really now? You asked me a question, so the presumption is that I was being presented with a choice."

"Your father asked me to recruit you."

That sharp jaw appeared again, and his eyes dulled some. "Did he now?"

"Are you too busy or something?"

"Yes. That's it." He took another step back and half-pivoted, like he was about to leave. "Let my father know."

"What? I can't do that."

"Sure you can."

"No." An icy panic began to rise in Willow's veins. She'd spent the last half hour of her morning off dreaming up a menu for the party, not to mention how she would coordinate the kitchen and have it all ready to serve at one time.

She snapped a look at Chance, ready to beg, when it occurred to her. "You're angry that your father hired your cousin, Rafael."

Chance pursed his lips, and, in a small way, Willow recognized Ace in him. "This subject is—"

"He didn't tell you about it ahead of time, did he?" Willow pushed herself up from the ground. She crossed her arms, considering him. "That's why you were upset the other day at breakfast."

"I wasn't upset."

"Grumpy then."

He sputtered out a sharp laugh. "Leave it be, Willow. This is of no concern of yours, all right?"

"Because I'm just the cook?"

"Because it's between my father and me."

She nodded. "As is my predicament ... between your father and me, I mean."

Chance let out a garbled groan, and Willow looked away. What was she doing confronting the boss's son like this? Had she lost her mind? He could have her fired, and then where would she be?

She blew out a breath and glanced around at the beautiful trees that framed the creek. If only life could be as simple and picture-perfect.

Truth was, Willow needed this job, not only for the money, but for the living arrangements it provided. Part of her compensation was the coziest, sweetest little cabin she'd ever seen. Already, it had become home to her, the place she laid her head each night and slept away her stresses.

She couldn't let anything happen to change that. That was that. Willow would have to find a way to make this party work with or without Chance's help.

She dropped her arms to her sides and took a step back, but Chance lunged toward her. She gasped as he wrapped his arms around her waist and tugged her so close she could see tufts of spiral hair sprouting from between the buttons of his shirt.

She attempted to yank herself from his arms. "What're you doing?"

"The creek!" He cinched her closer. If she weren't so outraged, she might've noticed the scent of cedarwood and earth wafting from him, and the unabashed strength that held her close.

Once they were a good foot away from the edge of the water, he let go of her waist. "You almost fell in."

"You mean you nearly pushed me in!"

Chance chuckled. He raised both hands like stop signs. "I saved you, darlin'."

Willow shook him off and ran her hands down the sides of her dress, as if brushing away both dirt and dignity. She needed to recapture the peace she had felt when walking out of church this morning. For the first time in months, she had not felt so … alone.

But that was before Ace piled on a big work assignment, and Chance refused to help her, then nearly toppled her right into the cold water of that creek!

Fine. Whatever. She would do this alone. No sense trying to pull help from an unwilling participant.

But Chance's voice interrupted her thoughts. "How many people at this … shindig?"

She picked up her bag from the ground and slung it over her shoulder, avoiding his eyes. "Forget it."

He touched the soft part of her upper arm until she looked at him. "How many?"

Willow swallowed before answering. "Your father says he expects about sixty-ish people." She paused. "Give or take."

Chance let out an incredulous whistle. He shook his head slowly, then peeled a look at her beneath his hat. "Sixty-*ish*, he said that, did he?"

"It's what he meant."

Chance snapped a look upward. "Fine."

"Fine, what?" The gold in his eyes settled on her. Stunning. That's all she could say about that …

"I'll help you."

Now it was her turn to hold up her palms. She added a decisive shake of her head. Willow had made up her mind—she did not want the assistance of an ornery, unwilling helper, something that would only slow her down and drop a stifling blanket over her party planning.

"He's testing you, you know," Chance said.

"Excuse me?"

"My father. He's testing you." Chance watched her. "He likes to haze new recruits."

"I don't think so. Plus, I've been here for a couple of months already."

He shrugged. "That's still new to my father."

"If he were testing me, as you say, why did he say I should get you to help me?"

He looked thoughtful for the first time since showing up here. "Because, darlin', he's testing me too."

Willow tilted her head to the side, watching for some sign that Chance was about to flash that cocky grin at her again. He didn't. "None of this makes any sense to me. Ace is a perfectly reasonable man ..."

Chance raised an eyebrow.

"You don't think so?"

"He can be reasonable, yes. But a man who has grown his ranch considerably from when he acquired it as a young man always does everything with a purpose in mind."

"And you think his purpose is to make you upset."

"I said he had a purpose—not that I knew what it was."

"Well, that's what I'd call interesting."

He grinned. "I'd call it annoying, but whatever you say."

Willow smiled. She crossed her arms at her chest and rocked back on her heels, looking fully into Chance's face now. She hadn't a clue about any of this testing nonsense, but her panic, though still present, had lessened considerably.

"Well, then, I guess we'd better put on a great party."

He grimaced, but nodded just the same. She couldn't tell if he cared one way or the other about the success of the party, but offered her his arm anyway and added, "At your service."

She was in over her head.

Chance could not shake the feeling that the beautiful young cook his father had hired without even a glance at her resume was about to go down in flames. Not that she didn't make a mean chicken pot pie. Or bacon omelet. Or any of the other mouth-watering meals he'd been served since she came here several months ago.

Oh, she could cook. But manage an event for sixty hungry bellies? Not an easy feat—that he could see. And it wasn't fair of Ace to ask it of her, especially on such short notice.

He found Willow in the kitchen in late morning, shoulders leaning over the island, her face buried in a cookbook.

"Anything I can help you with?"

She lifted her chin, her eyes unfocused. "Help ... me ... with?"

Chance plopped his hat onto the counter and scooted next to her. "You know, help you pick a menu?"

"A menu?"

He frowned. "You are trying to figure out what you'll be serving on Friday night, I presume."

She squinted, her mouth a straight line, then recognition came over her. Her hand brushed against his arm as she stood. "You're too late. I've already had all the fixins for Friday delivered." Willow opened the door of the long walk-in pantry and showed off the bulging shelves: cans of tomatoes, flour, yeast, nuts, olives, and more sat waiting to be used. She also lifted the door of the extra freezer stored in there and displayed an abundance of meat ready for whatever she was planning.

"Wow. You got all that into your pink car?"

"My car's not pink." She frowned. "I like to think of it as dusty rose. Or salmon, maybe."

"So is that salmon-colored toy street legal? Or just legally sad?"

"Mean."

He chuckled.

"At least she runs!" Mostly. And only after Willow whispers sweet nothings to it …

He stared at her, mouth pressed closed, but a smile fighting to get out.

She screwed up her lips. "Getting back to the party, and to answer the question hanging over your head, I'm planning to put it all in the smoker on Thursday."

"And stay up all night with it?"

"I can spray it all down late that night, you know, keep the moisture on it, and add more chips to it too. Should be fine until morning."

She'd … surprised him. That he would admit. When he'd walked in here to find her bent over a cookbook, lines etched across her forehead, Chance had expected to see panic in her eyes. She seemed to have it all under control, though.

"So I guess I'm off the hook."

She tilted a questioning glance at him. "Who do you think's going to tend to the smoker while I'm dishing up the sides? By the way, how are you with a knife?"

He frowned. Was that a trick question?

She continued. "Because I'm gonna need you to slice that meat thin enough to make sure we have enough to go around and thick enough for the crowd to hold their stomachs and moan about how they ate too much."

So maybe it wasn't the meal planning for the impending arrival of the prince and princess that had marred Willow's features. Whatever it was that caused stress lines to appear on her fresh-as-the-dew skin when he showed up in the kitchen, he would have to figure out.

Because, far as he could tell, it wasn't Friday night's extravaganza that had her fretting.

"I will be your sous chef on Friday. I'll stay by the smoker's side all night long if I have to."

"And get me in trouble with Ace? Not a chance." She pushed away from the island and fidgeted with her hands, pressing them together over and over. "No. To be sure, I'll need your help checking on that smoker, but you have a cousin to welcome into the fold. Far be it from me to get in the middle of all that."

Ah. So maybe the event was getting to her after all. No sense adding his feelings to the mix about the circus that he'd rather not attend. Somehow, he had to bury his thoughts while staying as emotionally uninvolved as possible.

It was going to be a long week.

Chance forced himself out of his headspace only to find her staring at him, one fist pressed into her side. "You're not thinking of doing anything crazy, are you?"

He frowned, shrinking back. "What are you suggesting?"

"Put cayenne pepper in Rafael's dessert ... salt in his lemonade"—she was ticking off ideas on her fingers, one by one—"a whoopee cushion on his chair ..."

Gently, he took her counting hand and moved it to her side. His fingers lingered on her skin, and he found himself caught between raw, sudden awareness of her and the palpable annoyance over the events of this week. "I will do what needs doing, and not a thing more."

A flicker of concern crossed her features, plunging questions deeper into Chance's psyche. He racked his brain for recollections, for the reasons why he did not know all that much about Willow.

Something akin to shame rolled through him. Maybe he hadn't paid any attention to her because he was caught up in … himself. Where did she come from all of a sudden, like a pretty light on a dark mountain?

"Well," she finally said as she gently extricated her fingers from his hand, "at least there's that."

He laughed, and the sound of it surprised him. "I'm glad you approve."

She darted a look at him, anything but approval on her face. Her eyes were hard, the lines in her forehead deep.

He tilted his head, examining her more closely. "Hey. You okay, Willow?"

She blinked. Then shook her head and pushed herself fully away from the island and began to putter with silverware in the sink. "Yes, of course." She flashed him a smile that he didn't quite buy. "Just a lot on my mind right now."

"Regarding the party?"

She stared at him for a beat, nodding slowly. "Yes. There are the usual meals to plan, plus, well, you know—all the rest." She flapped one hand in the air, then another. In a rushed voice, she added, "Oh, but don't mention anything to Ace. I've got it under control. No worries."

Chance gently wrapped his hands around hers, stilling

them in midair. "You've got this, Willow. It's just a party for a bunch of cowboys. They'll eat anything—"

"My food will be delicious."

He cracked a rueful look. "I have no doubt. But don't stress yourself over it. We don't want Rafael thinking life's going to be easy here on the ranch."

She narrowed her eyes.

"Stop that." He looked upward briefly. "I'm not planning to sabotage the guy."

"Your cousin."

"Right."

Willow pulled her hands to her sides, her mouth curled. "Thank you for the pep talk. I do appreciate it."

Chance sucked in his lip. Something was still not okay with her, but, frankly, he didn't care to think about Rafael and his impending arrival one more minute. He would have to bury any lingering questions about whatever was on Willow's mind. For now.

It was Wednesday afternoon, just two days before the big event, when Willow reread the message that had popped onto her phone screen a short time ago: her mama wanted to see her.

She hated to let this opportunity go by. Mainly, because her mother rarely asked for her by name anymore. When might this happen again?

But of all weeks! How would she make the time?

Kit McGinnis, the housekeeper, bounced into the kitchen just then, carrying a basket of laundry soaps, cleaning products, and towels. She dropped the whole mess on the island, blew a puff of air upward to dislodge a stray hair, and huffed a big, fat sigh. "I'm starved."

"Long day already?"

"The way Ace is fussin' about, you'd think royalty was daring to enter the premises this week."

Willow pushed away the impending detour in her schedule and pointed to a stool in front of the island. "Have a seat."

Kit turned a hopeful grin on her. "Don't tease me, Willow. I'm in no mood for teasin'!"

Willow flung open the door to the fridge and examined the contents inside. Something about a hungry soul needing sustenance buoyed her spirit, mainly because that was a need she could usually fulfill. Besides, it kept her mind off the myriad other things she had on her to-do list. She grabbed a plate, then pulled out lettuce, a bowl of chicken salad, and took fresh rolls from the pantry.

Kit gasped. "You're seriously going to feed me?"

"I am. All this is fresh too. Made it myself."

"Ooh, I can tell it's homemade. Smells so good."

Willow worked deliberately, slicing a roll and laying a curly red leaf on the bottom half, followed by a heaping spoonful of chicken salad. And then another. She topped it with the top half of the roll and pushed the plate in front of Kit.

Kit picked up the sandwich with gusto and took a bite. "Mm! Willow, honey, I think you're my new best friend."

If only. The last best friend she had left Willow behind, like all the lukewarm ones did. She was no longer looking for a bff, but she wouldn't turn down a trustworthy offer of one either.

With only a quick nod of acknowledgement, Willow busied herself with putting away the food, followed by wiping down the counter. Her delight in feeding the housekeeper some lunch was quickly squelched by thoughts she no longer cared to linger on.

"You okay over there?" Kit held the sandwich in front of her, as if in mid-bite.

"Me?" Willow shrugged. "Yes, yes, of course." She turned to the sink to squeeze water from the rag.

"Something's going on. My drama detector is up."

Willow coughed out a laugh. "Drama detector!"

Kit nodded. "It's more reliable than a cow at milking time."

"I seriously doubt that."

Kit frowned and looked upward, as if thinking. "Well, fine," she finally said. "But it's better than one of the cowhands at milking time."

Willow laughed and lowered her voice. "That I can see."

"I learned that one the hard way!" Kit said the words laced with laughter, but Willow had heard the gossip about how her romance gone bad with a ranch hand or someone led her straight into the arms of Eli, one of the hands who had been here the longest.

"Earth to Willow."

Willow met her gaze.

"You gonna spill it?"

The short answer: no. It would be all kinds of wonderful to have a friend to confide in, the kind she once had, before the events that turned her family's life upside down. She had to get the focus off her.

"Can I ask a question?" Willow said.

"Anything."

"I heard a rumor you once dated one of the hands, well, before Eli, I mean."

Kit raised one eyebrow and tilted her head, still chewing.

Willow's mouth went slack. What was she doing poking her head into someone else's business? So not like her! She'd only done it so she wouldn't have to answer any questions about herself …

Kit swallowed a bite. "You know it was Chance, right?"

Willow's eyes snapped open wide.

Kit laughed.

"Honey, that was in high school." She batted the air with a hand. "Water under the bridge.

"I-I'm so sorry. I shouldn't have been so nosy!" Willow turned away at the rush of heat in her face. She wiped her hands on a towel, letting them linger.

"Something tells me my high school love life isn't what's on your mind right now, cook."

Another text popped up on her phone then, but Willow slid it away from her view. She spun around and pasted on a smile. "I just have a lot to do this week. My mind's muddled with details for the party Ace is throwing."

"Let me help you."

Willow waved a hand at her. "Oh, you've got plenty to do, I'm sure! I'll—I'll be fine."

"Willow? I'm offering to help, so you should take me up on that. I may be a little older than you, young 'un, but I'm not a fake."

She had not expected Kit to be so direct. Since they'd met, she'd been funny and a little sarcastic, but their relationship had not crossed the line into any kind of enduring friendship. And Willow had been perfectly okay with that.

Kit dragged herself away from the counter. She

looked longingly at the empty plate in front of her, then snapped a look at Willow. "I'm here when you need me."

Willow managed a small smile, though she kept the guard around her heart intact. "Thank you so much.. I appreciate it, and, well ..."

"Yes?"

She shook her head. "Never mind. Was a crazy thought anyhow."

Kit stared at her, as if trying to figure out if she should say more. Eventually, she grabbed her basket and slid it off the counter. "Like I said, I'm here if you need me. Thanks for lunch!"

After she had gone, Willow stood silently for a good, long minute. She'd almost asked a favor of someone she barely knew, and the relief that flooded through her told her she'd made the right decision to change her mind.

What if ... she'd asked Kit to keep an eye on the kitchen for a time, and Ace questioned her about it? Or what if it annoyed Chance?

What if ... she'd asked Kit for help only to have to divulge why?

Absolutely not. Opening herself up for one question would lead to another, then another still. Thankfully, she had placed a tourniquet on the flood of questions before they even started.

Her phone buzzed. Probably one about her mother again. She snapped a look at the clock. If she left now, she could arrive back at the ranch in enough time to make the stew she was planning for supper.

She slid a tense look at her phone, but it wasn't a text at all. Instead, a voicemail appeared. Not surprising. Cellphone reception was an issue up here on this mountain, and she had missed a call more than once.

Hello, Ms. Mercer. This is Jack Landson. I'm calling to set up a time to check in with your mother, and I would like you to be there. Please call me at your earliest convenience. I would like to meet with her sometime next week. Goodbye.

Great. Exactly what she needed now. Sometimes it seemed as if the authorities had nothing better to do than make life rougher. Willow had long proved that her mother was no longer capable of chaos—really, she wasn't behind all that she'd been accused of—and that visits from someone like Mr. Landson would do more harm than good.

But her word wasn't enough. It was never enough.

Reluctantly, Willow stepped outside, far from the building. She crossed the driveway, then walked up around her small cabin, casting a sour glance at her tiny car. Chance was right—it did sort of look like a clown car. Oh, he didn't say so, but he didn't have to. With a sigh, she kept walking. She needed to make a phone call and to do so out of earshot of anyone on the ranch.

Chapter Three

The job had fallen to him. Chance stood in Sparky's old cabin and contemplated whether to leave the deer head on the wall and the bear skin rug in front of the fireplace.

He grinned. Wouldn't Rafael's sweet non-meat-eating wife love that?

Other than those two items, the cabin had been stripped bare by Eli and his men. Another ranch hand, one with plumbing skills, had replaced the toilet and sink in the bathroom and the rickety faucet in the kitchen. Otherwise, the place was in good shape. Hearty. Ready for many lives to fill its walls.

He took another glance around the place, including a look at the fireplace decor that any other foreman would love, and walked out to the small, fenced yard. Chance crossed his arms, sighing. From what he heard, Bella liked to garden, and here she would have a plot to tend.

Chance traversed the area, looking for gopher holes or other problems the couple might encounter. He kicked his boot at the sprinkler head shooting up from the earth, and it collapsed downward, as it should've when turned off. Chance scowled and considered his options. He could leave it that way for Rafael to fix. That was choice number one for him.

But his conscience always seemed to be on alert these days, redirecting his actions away from his thoughts.

He squatted down and unscrewed the cover of the sprinkler head. As suspected, the housing was filled with debris and dirt, which he loosened and cleared away with his fingertips.

"Good enough." He muttered the words as he replaced the cover and watched it slip into position as it was made to do.

Chance might have hopped onto his four-wheeler then and sped away if a voice hadn't caught his attention. He pulled the tip of his hat down, shading his eyes further, and stared into a small wooded area beyond the cabin, near where a grove of old olive trees sputtered along, alive despite the years of neglect.

Willow.

She was pacing, her phone to her ear, shoulders tense as she moved about. Not many realized that the wind that blew through that stand of trees often carried sound with it. Sparky liked to share the gossip he sometimes heard, and the guys never tired of hearing it around the campfire after a long day.

But listening in on a personal conversation wasn't his style. People deserve their privacy. He, too, coveted his own. Still, he had trouble tearing his eyes away from Willow, a certain sadness tugging at him at the way she paced, her chin tilted downward.

"See something you like?"

"What in the ...!" Chance spun around, his right hand

clenched, ready to pounce. Ace stood behind him, round eyes penetrating beneath the wide brim of his hat.

Busted.

"Sent you over here to make sure the cabin's in ship shape for Rafael and Bella—and their pipsqueak of a dog."

"There's an animal too?"

His father wasn't deterred. "But it looks like you've become distracted by some ... one."

"Not at all." Chance threw a nod to the cabin. "Just finished checking the hands' work in there."

"And?"

"It's ready. And so is the garden plot. Hopefully, the mutt won't dig it up." Chance pointed toward the sprinkler. "I fixed—"

Ace stared at him for a beat, his eyes shifting ever so slightly toward the earth. "Good. Your mother loved this little garden."

A slow smile found Chance as he nodded. "I remember. Mom loved all the small gardens around here."

"That she did." Ace quieted a moment, as if remembering. His eyes surveyed the land, the cabin, the grove of olive trees, and back to the small garden. "She always planted something special for incoming residents—rosemary bush here, some sunflower seeds there, whatever struck her fancy, depending on the time of year."

Chance nodded again. He remembered that, though he might not have had his father not pointed it out.

"So." His father broke the silence. "I'm here to see the place myself. Stick around, why don't you."

Chance stayed put, despite his desire to hop on that four-wheeler and head out to the pasture. He had animals to check on. And some thinking to do.

Instead, he found himself joining his father to wander into the spruced-up cabin, its wooden floors recently swept, its windowsills dusted, the faint scent of burnt smoke in the place. Ace stopped. He lifted his chin, his gaze laser-like on the deer peering back at him, dead as a doornail.

"Left it up there to welcome them, I suppose."

A smile played on Chance's face, but he tamped it down. "You said so yourself that you wanted to offer them a warm welcome."

Ace tipped his head toward his son. "The rug's a nice touch, though." After a brief silence, laughter bubbled up from him, followed by a cough, then a larger barrage of laughter.

Chance grinned. "I thought so."

Ace shook his head. "It's a good thing ol' Patsy isn't here anymore. Can't imagine what she'd say about throwing veggie burgers on the grill."

"Might have been worth it just to see her face."

"That it would."

"One thing's for sure"—Chance crossed his arms, still grinning—"never thought I'd hear the word veggie come out of your mouth."

Ace's grin widened. "Oh, come on now. In addition to flowers, your mama had a beautiful vegetable garden. I miss all that fresh stuff she made me eat."

Chance laughed. "There's something all three of her sons could agree on."

Ace pivoted, his expression serious again. "Need your expertise about something."

The abrupt change of subject was nothing new when it came to Ace. Chance's father could make merry in one moment and pound his fist on the table in the next. He wasn't a particularly volatile man, just someone who had always been rather difficult to read.

Something else Chance's brothers would back him up on.

"First, though, there's much planning still to do this week. You are helping Willow with the party for Friday evening, I take it?"

Chance's jaw tightened. "I am."

"Good." Ace kept his eyes trained on him for a few seconds, as if assessing his reaction. Then, "Stop by my office later this afternoon. I'd like you to review something in our books."

Chance straightened. He cleared his throat, about to reply. But Ace doffed his hat, silencing him, then turned to go. "I will see you later."

For once, Chance had no words. His father had always encouraged him to study numbers, to become educated about running a business from the financial end.

But after obtaining his degree, Chance had been nearly shunned for finding work far away from the ranch. Many times, after ordering supplies with the utmost care, he had offered to shepherd the ranch's finances, only to be rebuffed: *Stay in your lane, son. Stay in your lane.*

Finally, Chance had stopped asking.

After leaving numbers behind and returning home to reutilize the skills he'd learned as a kid—maintaining machinery, choosing the best milk-fed hay, building fences for the horses, etc.—it had made sense for Chance to immerse himself in his new life here.

Which is why the sudden hiring of his cousin to replace Sparky stunned him. Still so many questions in his mind. Why Rafael? Why not offer it to him first? Or maybe lure one of his brothers back?

Of course, the money wouldn't be an amount any of them had become used to. How could it? Still, there was sentimental value attached to the position. Chance had felt that from the moment he'd removed his dress shoes and tie, and replaced them with boots and one of his well-worn work shirts.

That was worth something.

Chance stepped outside, the midday sun's heat landing on him. His father's apparent change of heart was quickly replaced by a lingering thought: Willow.

He glanced toward the clearing again, wondering if she had found an answer to whatever dilemma had shaken her— and if there was anything he could do to help.

He would have to wait for an answer, though, because Willow was nowhere in sight.

Later that afternoon, Chance stepped inside the sunlit kitchen expecting to see dinner prep in full swing. Patsy always started around three o'clock, and a person had better have a good reason for showing up in her domain from that time until the meal was hot and served.

He wasn't in the mood for following orders, though. Not after showing up in Ace's office only to be asked to decipher a receipt for cattle cubes, rather than offer any significant advice on the ranch's direction.

His jaw flexed. Instead of the spice of chili or hint of smoky beef in the air, his senses ballooned with the aroma of … yeast.

Willow hadn't noticed him enter, her chin set with the

harsh line of determination, her mind seemingly a thousand miles away. Another difference from Patsy, who seemed to have eyes, ears, and even her nose attuned to the entry of dirty ranch hands clomping into her kitchen uninvited.

For a half-minute, Chase leaned against the doorframe and watched Willow, her sleeves rolled up, flour dusting her hands. He couldn't tell if this was the first time she'd made bread or the hundredth, but the way she sucked on her bottom lip and focused her eyes on the dough, he guessed the former.

"Smells good," he said, finally.

She startled, then plucked a pinch of dough and held it out to him. "Want a taste?"

Was she serious? Wouldn't that be … gross? He frowned, but pushed himself off the doorjamb and took one boot-shod step toward the island where she worked.

He reached for the dough.

Laughter poured out of her like stardust. His eyes turned to slits. She was laughing at him?

She brushed a wayward tendril of hair off her face with the back of one flour-dusted hand, still laughing. "Shoot. I wish I could've kept a straight face."

"Oh, yeah?" He kept trying not to smile, to maintain a stern expression.

"Yeah. I really needed your honest feedback." She gave him a deadpan expression.

A smile quirked the edge of his mouth, followed by a stifled laugh. It was no use. He hung his head, shaking it back and forth.

A sniffle escaped her, followed by a quick giggle. Their eyes met briefly before she dropped her gaze to a plate at the other end of the island. She nodded toward it. "As my penance for teasing you, go ahead and try one of those choco-late cookies I made for the party."

He spied the cookies piled high on a plate, his mouth watering, his stomach stirring.

She raised an eyebrow. "Unless you think that might spoil your appetite for dinner?"

His face was a dare as he swiped a cookie. "That was *never* a joke around here." He leaned against the counter that ran the length of the west wall and breathed in the scent of sugar, flour, and dark, rich chocolate. "Both my mother and Patsy would have chased us around with a fly swatter if we'd dared to ruin our appetites before the evening meal."

"Something tells me your be-hind collided with that swatter often."

"I beg your pardon?"

She tsked. He was enjoying this, and he didn't know whether to be relieved … or more careful to keep his distance. No matter how pretty the cook was, or how much he'd rather stick around to banter with her about, well, just about anything, there was work to be done.

He took a bite of a cookie. A scowl found his face.

She froze, sudden worry lines etching her forehead. "Is it bad?"

"Is what bad?"

"That delicious morsel you're crunching right now. Too much salt? Not enough sugar?"

His eyes slid to the half-eaten cookie in his hand, realizing he'd consumed half in one bite, his mind somewhere else. The beginnings of a grin quirked the edge of his mouth, but he wiped it away before polishing off the rest of it. He rubbed his hands together, letting the crumbs drop to the floor.

Willow followed them with her gaze.

The heat of something crept into his face. Chagrin, maybe? "Sorry, ma'am."

She shook her head and turned toward the sink. "Don't ma'am me." She grabbed a wadded-up towel and tossed it onto the floor.

It landed at his feet. He caught her gaze.

She gave one quick, pointed gaze toward the mess he'd left on the floor.

"You want me to …?"

"Unless you have a backache, yes."

Patsy wouldn't have put up with him either. She would've run him out of the kitchen with the first crumb drop. Might've given him a stern warning on his way out.

But one thing she would *never* do was make him clean it up.

He licked his lips, staring her down. Then he toed the rag with a booted foot, swirling it around the spot on the floor where it had landed.

Willow rolled her eyes, letting out a sigh. "Incorrigible." She snapped the towel up from the floor and spun it into the sink.

He chuckled. Hadn't felt the sound of laughter in his throat in how long? He couldn't remember.

"If you're finished now, I'd like to see how this bread comes out." She dumped it into a greased bowl and laid a tea towel over the top of it. When he didn't move, she flashed a look at him. "Just trying to get a head start on this weekend's festivities."

"Looks like more than a head start."

She let out a short laugh that didn't quite reach her eyes.

It surprised him to realize he could tell the difference. "I like to be prepared."

"Or maybe something else has got your attention today."

Her brows dipped.

"Saw you out by that stand of old olive trees." He spoke with a lowered voice.

"And?"

"Looked serious."

"You mean it sounded serious because you were—"

"Don't say eavesdropping. I don't do that."

"But you heard my conversation."

The lightness in her face faded away, bringing a twist to his heart. He hadn't meant to rile her, just … just what? *Keep your nose clean*, his father used to tell him whenever he'd leaned too far into his business about the ranch, especially when it came to the place's finances.

Is that what he was doing now? Being nosy?

Then again, if her troublesome conversation had something to do with the ranch, he ought to know about it. Was it a supply issue? A job offer somewhere else? He clucked his tongue and took a step back, remembering how his mother and Patsy used to laugh and carry on in the kitchen until he and his brothers came tumbling in.

He'd always thought it was because she doted on them, but maybe she was just trying to have a private conversation. Which means—he had overstepped. Chance turned to go.

Willow cleared her throat, stalling him. She forced a smile that was about as convincing as a rainstorm in the desert. "Just sorting out some personal stuff," she said. "Nothing to worry about."

Chance watched her for a beat, then nodded. Everybody

had their secrets. As long as they didn't affect the ranch, he had no right to them.

"Alright, then." He searched his head for a change of subject to chase away the awkwardness. "I don't suppose you're having car trouble or anything. 'Cuz if you are—"

"I'm not."

"One swift wind and that thing could go airborne."

Willow shoved a fist into her waist. "Did you really come here to insult my car?"

"Your comically tiny car."

She cracked a smile. "Stop it."

He cracked one back. "No, I did not come here to talk about *Lucille*."

She paused, looking upward, as if thinking. "Who in the world is Lucille?"

He shrugged. "Figured it was about time to give that pink puff of an automobile a name. Lucille fits her, I think."

"You're ridiculous."

"Now that we've established that ..."

Willow groaned.

"What I *really* came by to tell you, Miss Willow, is that I'm here to help when you need me. Can't imagine why Ace wants us to make such a big deal about the new recruit, but" —he shrugged, not wanting to talk about it all that much— "I'm here to help. Call on me *if you want*."

Her eyes held doubt, but she said, "You mean that?"

"I said I'd help, didn't I?" He hadn't meant for that to sound so harsh. Even to himself, it had.

A slow, skeptical smile pulled at the corner of her lips. "Then grab an apron, cowboy. We've got a party to plan."

Well. Chance had helped her all right, but the start of a grin she'd seen on his face earlier in the week when she'd forced that flower-patterned apron on him had turned to a flat line the minute Rafael and his sweet wife, Bella, showed up.

Oh, and that dog! What had Seabiscuit, Bella's cute Pomeranian-mix pup, ever done to Chance?

He wasn't mean or anything, but he did ignore the poor little thing who nose bumped the cowboy's boot. The dog didn't give up, though. Bumped him again for good measure, then let out a bark that said, *Play with me!* Somehow, Seabiscuit sensed he was going to have to work extra hard to get that grumpy ol' cowboy on board with his presence here at the ranch.

As far as Willow was concerned, the precious animal could clean up her kitchen floors any time he liked. She loved dogs but hadn't been able to have one in her life for years. Not with all the uprooting that had taken place.

"You've outdone yourself, cook!" Bella appeared in the kitchen, her face flushed, her smile bright. Seabiscuit peeked out from the carrier slung around her shoulder. "The barn looks and smells amazing. I am overwhelmed by all of it. Truly."

Willow tossed a damp towel over her shoulder and smoothed a hand across her forehead where a bead of perspiration threatened. "Bella Sutter, scoot! You're a guest of honor tonight."

Bella laughed. "I'm content to leave that honor to my husband, but thank you."

Willow leaned toward the pup and chucked him under the chin. I suppose you could stay to help me mop the floors later, friend."

"Ahh, he would love that, but what can I do to help now?"

"No-nothing. Really." Willow straightened. Her voice broke, and she swallowed back a sudden lump in her throat. What in the world?

The truth was, she was tired—both mentally and physically. She'd done her best not to show how overwhelmed she'd been with not only handling the normal kitchen duties, but planning this party as well. With all Chance's stomping around here this week, you'd have thought Miranda Priestly from *The Devil Wears Prada* was moving in instead of the sweetest woman she had likely ever met.

"Oh boy, I didn't mean to upset you."

Willow shook her head tightly. The last thing she needed right now was to tip anyone off to her family problems. It hadn't helped that Landson had called again. She had followed her mother up into these mountains overlooking the sea for logistical reasons, but the strain of keeping up her responsibilities--all while keeping her family life private—had become a mountain all its own.

The word "secretive" came to mind, but since when did

family troubles require airing publicly like so many do on social media? She had carefully scrubbed her accounts years ago and only kept one alive, under her initials, to keep an eye on her uncle.

Unfortunately, he hadn't been too active lately, which was a good thing. Or maybe he was just trying to be on his best behavior and not draw any attention to himself.

Sigh.

An all-too-familiar commotion from the mudroom broke the friendly banter. Chance's voice preceded him into the long and narrow kitchen. "You have *got* to be kidding!"

"Something wrong?" Willow asked to be polite, not because she cared all that much to hear any bad news.

Chance's handsome mug was less than when wearing that scowl on it. He opened his mouth, but it froze there as his eyes settled on Bella's presence in the kitchen. His expression morphed in a way that Willow was beginning to recognize—from spitting mad to a flash of sarcasm to, finally, *get ahold of yourself, man.*

"Bella," he said, doffing his hat, his voice polite.

"Hey, Chance." She bounced Seabiscuit in that sling like a newborn. Probably nervous. And why wouldn't she be? Chance barreled into the place with fire lighting him up, only to turn the flame down when he'd been caught by an outsider.

Guess that made Willow an insider.

"What's got you in a snit?"

He slid a look at her. "Rain."

Willow gasped. "It's not supposed to be here until tomorrow!"

"Yeah, well, tell that to the weather app." He tapped his phone, the lines at the corners of his eyes pulled tight.

"Clouds rolling in, and that old barn's roof has been needing replacing for years."

Willow nodded, and now it all made sense. She'd heard Ace and Chance arguing about that very thing soon after she'd arrived here, but never learned if they had made a decision whether to repair it anytime soon.

She swallowed. "It's the reason it's been empty for so long, isn't it?"

Chance nodded, his jaw taut.

"Look—the clouds are already blowing away." Bella pointed out the window over the sink. "It's all going to be okay. Don't you worry, Chance."

He strode toward the window, muttering "Let me see that …" under his breath.

All three sets of eyes focused on the dance of clouds against a shadowy blue sky. The threat of rain hovered, but as Bella said, the clouds flitted away as quickly as they had come.

Willow clapped her hands, then brushed her fingers in the air toward them both. "Shoo. The both—I mean, all three of you." She gave Seabiscuit a quick pet. "We can't worry about what the weather's thinking about right now. I've got to get the rest of the food out. Chance? Please send the boys in for the trays, okay?"

"I'll just stay here and—"

She shook her head and took a step toward him, walking Chance backward. Bold of her, but with so much on her shoulders, she didn't care. Second time she'd nearly over-stepped with her boldness this week. Gave her pause because she needed this job.

But she also needed peace and focus in the kitchen. She continued, "You've done enough for now. Go on." She handed him a fat pitcher of lemonade, her specialty. "Send the boys back, and maybe later you can help us tear it all down."

"But ..."

Chance must've recognized the flash in her eyes that told him it was no use. She wasn't going to budge. It wasn't that she couldn't use the help. She could. But today was important to Ace. She'd seen it in the way he contemplated the pasture, the barn, and the cabins, and looked longingly at the horse paddocks. So much pride.

And, honestly, Ace looked tired to her lately, likely weary over battles with his son. So, decision made. No more drama in the kitchen. Not tonight. Not on her watch.

Tonight would be perfect.

She'd done it.

The aroma of smoked brisket, warm cornbread, and yeasty rolls curled through the old barn, inviting guests into the cozy, lit space like a comforting embrace. Smokeless tea lights flickered on every tabletop, their golden glow glinting off Mason jars filled with fresh-cut lupine, daisies, and asparagus fern. A soft hum of music played in the background, while laughter echoed off the rafters.

Chance had to admit—though he'd never say it out loud —the place looked better than it had in years. Alive, almost. Like it had a soul again.

He leaned against a support beam near the barn door, arms folded, and cast a halfhearted glance over the crowd. Most folks were gathered near the long food tables, swapping ranch stories and slathering butter onto hot slabs of corn-bread. Rafael stood near the doublewide entrance, shaking hands and grinning like he'd never left this place behind. Bella stood poised beside him, perky, smiling, and gracious. Together, they looked comfortable. Settled.

Like they belonged.

A sudden clench to his jaw caught Chance off guard. A knot twisted in his gut as he watched Rafael's gaze sweep across the ranch, taking it all in. Like he owned the place.

A warm breeze drifted in, carrying with it a distant rumble from somewhere far across the mountain range. It began as a low pulse, maybe just a truck downshifting on the road beyond the ridge. Depending on the wind's direction, sounds like those could whimper … or roar.

Willow's voice broke into his thoughts. "You look ready to punch someone."

Chance blinked. She stood beside him, eyebrows raised, a quirk to her lips. Hair piled loosely on her head, and a few strands curling around her face. Her eyes drooped, soft circles forming beneath them. She was tired, no doubt about that, but … beautiful.

He looked away, his voice flat. "I'm being friendly."

"Maybe open your hand before you cut off your circulation." He turned his face, and she nodded to his balled-up fist.

Chance blew out a sharp breath and ran a hand down his cheek, a beard starting to fill in now. "I'm fine."

She paused, watching him. "You sure?"

"I. Am."

Willow gave him a look that said she didn't quite believe his retort, then gestured with her chin toward the tables. "Well, that wall doesn't need you to hold it up." Her tone had softened some. "Go mingle. Grab some lemonade before Ace sees you scowling in the corner like a spooked steer."

Chance huffed a laugh. "And if I don't?"

"Then you'll break ol' Ace's heart." She smirked, turning to flag down one of the ranch hands.

A hand passed by with a tray of rolls. Chance snagged one, and Willow's eyes narrowed playfully.

She stopped the tray with a touch. "Hang on. These look like they were thrown together by a couple of blindfolded raccoons." With deft hands, she rearranged the rolls into a symmetrical pattern. "I leave for one second, and the kitchen falls apart."

Chance chuckled under his breath. "Sounds like job security."

Willow glared at him. The corner of her mouth twitched, and she nodded toward the middle of the barn. "Go get yourself something to drink, cowboy."

He pushed away from the wall, muttering as he went. "Anything you say, darlin'." Out of her earshot, he whispered, "Wouldn't want to disappoint the family."

"You sayin' something, son." Ace had entered the barn. Chance became vaguely aware of his father's diminishing height.

He cleared his throat. "Was just telling Willow this place looks better than it has in years."

Ace waited a beat, then flicked his gaze through the expansive place. He nodded. "I would have to agree with you there."

"Can I get you a drink?"

"Nothing for me now. I'll wait here to greet some of our guests."

Chance nodded his acknowledgment, then he strode

toward the flower-laden refreshment table. Another low rumble stirred through the floorboards. Barely noticeable. But it was there.

In hindsight, Chance shouldn't have drunk that lemonade.

Not that it was Willow's fault. Eli must've spiked it when she wasn't looking—he'd seen it, even smirked when it happened. He could've warned someone. Could've picked something else. But he hadn't. Maybe part of him wanted a reason to feel off-kilter.

Now, he was paying for it.

The barn felt stifling, the lights too bright. Laughter bounced off the walls with a hollow clang. Boots clomped to the music, oblivious to the bitterness pooling under his tongue. Would this night never end?

Willow moved like a wind current through the crowd, checking platters, exchanging pleasantries, keeping everything humming along. But when Willow's eyes found his, the look she gave him was anything but friendly.

She marched across the worn wooden floors, brow furrowed, eyes laser sharp. If she were a bobcat, he'd be waving his arms like a beast to deflect the attack.

"You've had enough," she said under her breath, leaning over him. Her presence teased his senses. He pulled himself upright, not because he cared to mingle, but to take in more of her.

"I—" Chance started, but the words felt thick, heavy in his throat.

"You're gonna make a mess of things," she hissed.

Again.

He hadn't heard the word, but he felt it. The disappointment in her tone wrapped around him tighter than a noose. He heard it in his mind, coming from Ace too.

"I'm not drunk," he murmured. "Just … off."

Willow tilted her head, watching him with those deep, dark eyes that missed nothing. "Your color is bad," she whispered. "You're sweating. And the floor—Chance, do you feel that?"

He blinked hard. The floor did feel all wrong, like it was shifting under him. But not because of the lemonade. Something deeper. A hum. A pressure shift.

"I think …" he began, but then staggered slightly as a tremor vibrated through the barn's structure.

A crash behind him drew startled cries. A tray hit the floor, shattering glass and splashing lemonade across his boots. A few guests stumbled, grabbing for balance.

"What in the—" someone shouted.

"Chance!" Willow reached out as he braced himself on the edge of a table. The barn walls groaned with an eerie creak, timbers flexing with the force of wind—or something.

It wasn't the drink. It wasn't a dizzy spell.

An earthquake, and what sounded like a storm, had come. All rolled into one.

He looked at Willow again, and for a split second, that wasn't pity he saw in her eyes—but fear. Real fear.

The earth's tremor passed in under ten seconds, but the

stillness it left behind cast the barn in an eerie hush. High-pitched voices punctuated the air.

Was that an earthquake?

That was a big one!

Wonder where it was centered?

Whoa! Are those lights swingin'?

The questions were customary. Californians didn't panic after earthquakes—usually. Instead, a flurry of questions and internet searches usually followed a shaker. And aftershocks.

Chance listened for one of those, the hammering in his chest slowing some when it didn't come. His eyes scanned the crowd that he suddenly felt responsible for. Lights flickered, while others stayed solidly lit.

Willow touched his arm. "You okay?"

Chance gave a short nod, jaw tight. "Wasn't the lemonade."

They shared a look. Though the jolt didn't seem to have caused any damage, some of the guests, especially the older ones, walked stiffly, as if on edge.

Another low rumble rolled through the place, but this one was different. It came from overhead, rushing through the vaulted barn with a howl and a whistle.

Wind.

And, then, rain.

Lots and lots of rain.

No way.

Chance pushed the barn door open to the cacophony of rainwater coming down in sheets.

"Man!" Eli joined him. "That's a gully washer, all right."

A massive gust drove the rain sideways, slicing through the open doorway like a waterfall showerhead on full speed.

The sudden flush of water and wind soaked the entryway, causing guests to leap backward for shelter.

Chance pushed the door partway closed again and stepped back, considering. Then came a single drip.

He looked up. The roof groaned. The leak widened, creating a pattern that zigged and zagged its way toward unsuspecting guests.

Willow leaped toward a tray of cornbread, gasping as water drops began to fall.

Chance raised both hands in disbelief. "Fantastic."

Outside, the rain continued to hammer the gravel and dirt beyond the doors, an unwelcome sight to guests watching it fall, their cars a long, muddy hike away.

As they stood there under what might have otherwise been a cozy, rainy day, a flash of lightning lit the treetops. An aggressive gust blew in another sheet of rain, accompanied by thunder. Guests groaned, and murmurs of disbelief crowd-surfed through the barn.

Chance shoved the door fully closed. He spun around, addressing everyone, his arms open wide, "All right, everyone. It's time to move. The main house is warm—and open to everyone."

He sent a pointed glance at Willow, who nodded her agreement. "I've got scones and lemon bars inside!"

Chance responded with a nod. This old roof wasn't going to hold if the wind kicked up. He had to get them inside. Willow knew that too.

"Hear that, everyone? Scones and lemon bars!"

He caught Rafael's eyes. "Lead the front group."

"Yes, sir. I'll get the coffee on once I'm inside."

He nodded, then to Eli, he said, "You'll help me."

"You got it."

Chance clapped his hands, ignoring the fat droplet of water that landed on the brim of his hat before falling onto his hand. "Amazing! Our plan is set. You all go inside quickly and get dry and warm. Eli and I will help anyone who needs assistance. Let's all stay safe—no running in high-heeled boots!"

That sent laughter through the barn.

Chance shoved the door open fully again, and Rafael waved guests through.

Quickly, Chance assigned Eli a group, then he took the other. He snagged a couple of hands to help, making sure someone was on either side of Miss Helen, who hadn't missed a Sutter Creek gathering in thirty years.

Ace appeared, shoulders hunched against the spray, just as Chance brought up the rear. Water saturated the old man's face, and Chance grabbed a towel from a nearby table and pressed it into his father's hands.

Ace took in Willow, who guided several to safety. He swung his chin back to Chance again and gave him a single, sharp nod.

Chance nodded back.

Rain poured across their path as they made their way to the grand portico with columns flanking the entry to the main house. Once everyone had made it inside, Chance spun around.

Willow's eyes searched his face.

"Go on. Get inside," he said.

She sidestepped him. "You going back?"

"Have to. The barn needs battening down."

"I'm going with you."

He shook his head, but she stopped him with a touch on his arm. "Scones and lemon bars are laid out. Kit and Bella are serving them up."

His eyes searched her face. She *wanted* to go back out into that mess?

She squeezed his arm tighter, and he rolled a look to the heavens. "Fine," he said with a quick shake of his head. "C'mon." Then he took her hand and they sprinted back to the barn.

Together, they discarded empty plates and cups, stacking them up in gray, rubber bins. They dragged tarps over tables they hoped to salvage once the storm was over, and gathered up belongings, such as sweaters and scarves that guests had left behind.

"Here." He tossed her someone's phone.

She glanced at the screen. "By the screen saver with Rafael's face on it, I'm guessing Bella left this behind."

Chance rolled his eyes. "Maybe he has a picture of himself on that phone."

"Please."

He chuckled. "Don't 'please' me."

She chided him with a look that would have made Patsy proud. So much so that he snapped his gaze away under the heat of it. The rain had not let up. He cleared his throat. "We need to go."

She nodded, and followed him outside, keeping her head bowed. As wind whistled through gaps in the walls, they pushed the barn door closed, with Chance adding a brace for good measure.

He turned to Willow. Saturated, loam-colored strands of hair framed her face. Smudges of mascara rested beneath her eyes. He leaned toward her. "Ready?"

She shrugged, her smile back now. "As I'll ever be!"

They spilled into the main house, wet clothes plastered to

their skin, and smelling of wood smoke and fresh air, earth and pine. If guests minded—or noticed—they didn't let on.

Rafael was ladling reheated chili into bowls, while Eli handed out mugs of hot coffee. About a dozen guests had gathered around the television in the den off the primary living room, getting up-to-the-minute reports of the storm's damage.

Willow peeled off her apron and hung it on a hook in the mudroom. Chance hovered a moment, as if about to say something, but Willow nodded toward the kitchen.

"Your cousin stepped up," she said.

He nodded, closed-mouthed. Then, "That he did."

Willow's voice was a whisper now, her gaze imploring. "I understand the desire for a second chance."

Under different circumstances, he might have dug deeper into Willow's statement. What second chance was she seeking? Or had she sought? Yet, she'd been talking about Rafael, as if to say, he's not the enemy. Felt like it sometimes, but then again, when he really thought about it, Rafael had lost a lot in his lifetime.

That was something Chance could relate to.

He turned back to respond, and Willow had disappeared. He made his way into the kitchen and clapped Rafael on the shoulder. "Any of that left for me?"

Rafael raised his brows, but handed him a bowl, the steam still coming off of it. "You bet."

Chance took his meal into the living room, where he found Ace in his leather recliner, wrapped in a wool blanket and observing the guests milling about. A group of women had gathered around the fireplace where flames licked the air.

"Aren't you hungry?" Chance asked him.

Ace did not respond at first, but his eyes never left his son.

Willow appeared, offering Ace a bowl of chili, but he waved her off. She cast a wordless gaze at Chance before delivering the bowl to a guest sitting by the fire.

"Warm enough?" Chance nodded at the blanket on Ace's lap.

His father pursed his lips, nodding.

Chance took a bite of chili, savoring the blend of chili powder and steak. He stabbed his fork into the bowl, letting it stand there. "Well, Ace, you sure know how to throw a party."

"If this is your way of proving you're planning to stick around, leave the monsoon out next time," Ace said straight-faced.

"What can I say? I'm a powerful guy."

Willow swept back in again, this time with a mug of coffee for Chance. She handed it to him. "Hey there, Mr. Powerful. This should help warm you up."

He raised a brow at her.

Willow blinked, like he'd caught her off-guard with a look.

Chance held her gaze. "You okay?"

She licked her lips. "Sure was a mess out there."

"Yeah." He cracked a grin at her. "We handled it."

"You handled it. I was just your ... lackey."

His expression split into a grin.

Willow smiled and lowered her voice. "By the way, cowboy, if the goal was to prove you can lead, even when dinner is floating away in a flood ..."

"Nailed it, didn't I?"

She looked up at him, her eyelashes glistening, a conciliatory smile on her mouth. "You did," she said. "You really did."

Outside, rain pounded against glass, while inside a fire crackled in the hearth, cared-for guests chattered in low voices, and a bustling kitchen kept the party going. For his part, Ace snoozed in his chair, oblivious to the adrenaline rush still surging through his insides.

And then ... the reality of what had occurred tonight hit Chance like a blow torch. The unplanned-for storm. Faulty infrastructure. Chaos. And now, everyone lounging around like this was normal. Like this night ended the way it was meant to.

If that were so, why did he suddenly feel the threat of suffocation?

Willow turned before heading to the kitchen, and once again, their gazes met. She leaned toward him, as if to ask him something, but he turned away and strode out of the room without a word.

Chapter Five

At dawn the next morning, Willow slipped out of her cottage and into "Lucille." She rolled by the main house, which showed no sign of stirring. But, just in case, she'd set the timer on the coffee pot and placed a basket of rolls and scones on the island.

The kitchen could wait an hour or so, giving her an opportunity to think. And breathe. The cleanup, the meeting with her mother's parole officer, well, there would be plenty to face when she returned.

She wound her way down the hill, past walnut and oak trees, their long limbs stretching across the road. The town still slumbered as she rolled by, until down the winding hill, the view gave way to open ocean.

Minutes later, she pulled into a spot at the curb and watched as day broke from the east, casting a golden glow across the water.

She let out a sigh. Despite the stress of her mother's situation—and condition—and the absolute anarchy from last night's storm, her lungs relaxed. The sound of the sea filled her mind, replacing the quiet and steadiness of the mountains.

Despite the worries, how fortunate was she? To live this close to the sea, but be able to fall asleep listening to mountain birds and the sway of trees outside her small cottage.

The contrast had not escaped her. While the mountains provided quiet and steadiness, the sea rolled and danced. The salt air cleansed the air around her, and the rushing sound of the waves?

Healing.

Until that first breath of briny oxygen had hit her lungs, Willow had not realized just how wound up she had been. Tension melted out of her. The intense week of preparation she'd just endured, followed by last night's sudden earthquake and storm … she shook her head. Was it all just a dream?

And yet, somehow, all the pieces and loose ends, the detour from careful execution to a mad scramble, had all come together. Adrenaline had a way of making the mind forget that all you want to do is crawl into bed and swaddle in the covers.

She sank into deep sand on a natural dune just above the shoreline. A wave rolled onto wet sand. Last night, guests had hunkered down in the great room, eating, mingling, and some dozing. Eli entertained with his jokes. Rafael and Bella, who could've escaped to their cabin, didn't. Instead, Bella chatted with guests with little Seabiscuit peeking out of her front pouch, while Rafael stoked the fire, making sure the place was as inviting as it was warm.

And Chance.

She bit back a smile, remembering how he stepped up. Steady, sure, undeterred … and, oh, he smelled so good through all of it. Like smoke and vanilla and hard work. No complaints, just his presence—and his gaze.

Theirs had collided more than once. Was it the frenzy of night that had caused the ripple running through her whenever they'd caught eyes?

The tiny smile on her face dimmed with the turn of her thoughts. If it weren't for his sudden change of mood at the end of the evening, she might have thought … well, she wondered what had been on his mind before then.

She hugged her knees to her chest, watching that golden glow from behind her spread across the water. Waves crested, rolled, then quietly stretched their way toward her. In the distance, a lone surfer paddled further out where the waves began their rise. It took him a few tries, but eventually he caught something rideable, carving a clean line toward the shore.

She straightened, squinting for a better view. He was out there without a wetsuit, and she shivered. He moved with strength, precision, and never wavered until the break. He turned back around, paddled out, then turned abruptly when another wave rose.

She watched him catch it without hesitation, then ride it in. And she knew. He dropped the board on the sand, retrieved a towel, and rubbed it through his dark hair.

Their eyes met. No scowl on Chance's face today, but instead a sort of peace that caused a tumble in her heart. His surprise spread easily to a grin, and he dipped his head in her direction, as if wearing an imaginary hat.

Can't get the cowboy out of the surfer …

He hooked the towel around his neck and held the ends of it like weights. Thoughts she wasn't ready for invaded her mind, a need to understand what drove him. She pushed them aside as he approached.

"Hey."

"Hey, yourself."

"This your usual spot?" His voice was soft, earnest. "Don't think I've ever seen you here before."

Usual spot? She hadn't had one of those in years. She smiled. "I do come here occasionally, but honestly, I don't have much time. Wish I did."

He looked out to sea before swinging his chin back her way. "Here"—he reached a hand down to her—"let me help you up."

His hand was warm and strong, and if she thought about it too much, she might realize he held on for a beat longer than necessary.

They stood shoulder to shoulder, watching the waves curl toward the shore. Finally, she said, "You took off last night." She didn't mention that, just before he left, his eyes had turned dark, as if a new storm brewed behind them.

He didn't move. "You expected me to stick around?"

Yes. No. Sort of. It wasn't that she thought he *had* to stick around; he'd surely done plenty to make sure they were all safe and provided for last night. But ... it was the abruptness in his departure that she couldn't shake.

"I, well ..."

"If it makes you feel better, I escorted people to their cars after the rain stopped. Checked on the mess of guys passed out in the great room after midnight. Put out the fire." A faint smile tugged at the corner of his mouth, but it didn't quite reach his eyes. "Did I miss anything?"

"Nope." She swallowed, ignoring his sarcasm. "I don't suppose they're all still asleep."

"Like they've been flattened by a tornado."

"Oh!" She turned around. "I should probably get back—"

Chance stopped her, his hand lightly on her shoulder. "They'll survive. Probably raiding the leftovers as we speak."

"So, you got up early and had to tiptoe around them all?"

He was quiet for a moment. "Would've if I'd ever gone to bed in the first place."

She gasped. "Chance!" She searched his face. "Tell me you didn't stay up all night."

His stony expression told her that he had, indeed, not laid his gorgeous head on his pillow last night. If he'd been out in the barn, resetting everything, it probably looked better than it had at the start of the party.

Willow leaned to the side, taking in Chance's faraway expression. "You okay?" she asked softly.

Chance didn't answer right away. "Just thinking," he said finally.

"Dangerous habit."

"I agree with you there."

Neither spoke for a long while, but she had questions. Nothing about it felt awkward, and if she were honest, Willow wished she could stay all day.

"You ever get the feeling that you're trying to fill every gap," he murmured, finally, "but it's never enough?"

Willow's breath caught. Of all the things he could've said … "I think I feel that way every day."

He turned to look at her then, vulnerability in his eyes. "I'm up before dawn most mornings. I know every line of the ranch's irrigation map, the fenceposts that lean when the wind shifts from the north, which hay bales are best for which horses. I'm the guy folks come to when something's broken, or busted, or in need of fixing, but still—"

"You're not the foreman," she finished for him.

Chance's mouth was grim. "Don't care about that."

"But?"

"Rafael shows up, and Ace throws him a welcome party and hands him a title. I've been here for years. And somehow, I'm still just ... here."

"You want to know your place."

"Didn't say that." His voice turned gruff.

"You didn't have to."

A silence stretched between them. The sun pushed a little higher from the east, painting the edges of the sea in gold. Somewhere in the distance a gull called out once, then again.

"I'm not just a hand. I'm not the boss. I'm not the new blood or the old guard. I'm just one of the sons who left." Chance kept his gaze out to sea. "And has never been forgiven for it."

Willow stood still, feeling the heat radiating from him. Her voice was quiet, steady, though she didn't know what to fully make of what he'd just confessed. "Maybe they don't know what to call you because you don't know either."

He turned his head slowly toward her, droplets of water cascading down his forehead. For a moment, neither of them moved.

"You trying to say something, Willow?"

She shrugged, though her throat tightened. "I'm just saying maybe what matters isn't what they call you. It's what you answer to."

He watched her, as if weighing her words against some unspoken ache.

Then, slowly, he stepped around to stand in front of her. His bare toes bumped hers, and when he stopped, he stood so close she could see a faint bruise forming beneath his jaw where he must've caught an elbow or the corner of a metal tray in the rush to escape last night's storm.

"You know what I'd like to be called?" His voice turned low and rough like gravel.

Willow's heart pounded. "What?"

He leveled his gaze on her, but made no move forward. He didn't touch her, but the tension between them made her think, for just an instant, that he wanted to.

"Trusted."

The word landed like a soft knock on a heavy wooden door. Willow searched his face. Not because she didn't believe him, but because she did—and it undid something inside her.

She wanted to reach for his hand, to let her fingertips say what her voice couldn't. But she knew her place. He was the boss's son, and though she might give him grief in her kitchen, tell him not to keep slamming her fridge door, she was not about to cross the unmistakable, invisible line between them.

Instead, she said something she felt down deep. "You already are, Chance. I know it."

He ran a hand across his chin, but he didn't step back.

Neither did she.

The silence between them landed differently now, like the moment right before dawn breaks over a foggy hill, when you're not sure if the sun is coming, but you think it could.

A salty breeze stirred the air between them, warmer than when she had arrived. The burdens she'd brought with her this morning seemed lighter too.

The glass doors of the Topa Mountain Care Home needed cleaning. Always her first thought each time she pushed her way into the lobby of the small facility.

Her second thought was whether that fact presented a foreboding about her mother's care. Would they ignore her the way they always seemed to ignore that front door's glass?

The sharp burn of antiseptic that hit her sinuses as she stepped inside was, in some way, a relief. Cleanliness being next to godliness wasn't actually in the Bible, but as Willow scrubbed the Sutter kitchen each day, she thought it ought to be.

The care home was tucked along a leafy stretch of road just four miles from the ranch. When she'd found this job, so close to her mother's residence, she took it as a sign from the Almighty himself that everything was under his control.

Inside the building, she instinctively reached inside her puffy jacket pocket. The envelope was still there—inside, a progress report, notes from her mother's last wellness check, and a folded copy of the parole schedule. Everything Mr. Landson would ask about.

Her fingers brushed against the soft cotton lining of her pocket, and—for just a moment—she wished she could leave it all here. Just be the cook at Sutter Creek Ranch. Just plan meals and fill plates and learn Chance's quirks without worrying that one wrong move would unravel everything.

But that wasn't her life. It hadn't been for a long time.

The staff member in the lobby greeted her with a nod.

They knew her by now. She handed the woman a plate of molasses cookies. She smiled and hugged them to her.

"Mr. Landson's in the family room," the woman said, gesturing toward the east wing while still holding onto the plate. "He said to send you straight back."

Willow smiled politely, keeping her head low as she made her way down the corridor. She passed a nurse adjusting a resident's blanket, the soft murmur of television coming from a partially open door, and finally reached the room with the wide windows overlooking the garden.

Jack Landson sat at a square table near the glass, his iPad open. He looked up when she entered, offered a conciliatory smile, and motioned for her to sit.

"Appreciate you coming, Ms. Mercer."

Willow slid into the chair opposite him, laying her handbag on her lap. "Of course."

Landson studied her for a moment, then turned and began to scroll through his notes. "Your mother's doing well, overall. No incidents logged in the last six weeks. Her medication's on track and therapy sessions consistent."

Willow nodded, exhaling quietly. "She seems calmer lately."

"Stability helps," he said. "So does a predictable environment. I'm glad you agreed to move her here. How has your transition been?"

"Straightforward. I think we both like it here."

He nodded.

"It's just …"

One brow rose. "Yes?"

She leaned forward. "My mother has always hated feeling, you know, confined."

He removed his glasses and laid them on the table.

"Being here is a condition of her parole, Willow. And you've made it clear that you want to keep her close. That's working, for now. But we do have to review her status every quarter."

Willow leaned forward, hands clasped in her lap. "Is something wrong?"

Landson tapped the pen against his notepad. "Not wrong, no. But her name came up in a routine audit. A note from six years ago mentions your uncle. There was a warning to avoid contact."

Willow's breathing hitched.

Landson glanced up. "Are you aware of any recent attempts by him to reach out?"

"No," she said quickly. "No, he hasn't contacted her."

"You sure?"

"I would know." Her voice was firm now. "He doesn't know where she is. And I've made certain he never will."

There was a pause. Landson watched her as if she were testifying on the witness stand.

"I assume you'd notify us immediately if something changed?"

Where was this all coming from? She glanced out the window, her mouth going slack. Everything had been carefully planned. Her mother's care, her move to be closer to her. The truth was, Willow had been counting down the days until her mother could be fully released from scrutiny.

Yet, what she would do at that point was anyone's guess.

One thing she had not counted on, nor planned for, was the re-entry of her uncle—her mother's brother—back into their lives. Not after all he'd done.

"Willow?"

She turned abruptly away from the window. "I would

notify you. Certainly. But my uncle is not part of our lives anymore. I'd never allow it."

Landson tapped something into his iPad. "Excellent. Following protocol here. When families are involved in the original offense, the parole board becomes quite inquisitive."

Family. A foreign word to her, at least in the standard sense. She'd always wondered what those big families were like, the ones with many children, a big home, and lots of chatter around the dinner table.

Of course, those could fall apart and be a place of sadness too. She saw that in the Sutter family. Ace and Chance at odds, two sons who rarely visit, and the years lost to bitterness where Rafael was concerned.

Willow kept her face still, unreadable.

"How's your job?" he asked after a beat.

She blinked. "At the ranch?"

"Yes. I gather it's pretty demanding."

"It is," she said. "But it's honest work that I'm grateful to have found."

"And it keeps you close."

"Yes, right." She'd said that already.

He gave her a long look, eyes peering over the top of black reading glasses. She thought he had something more to say, then abruptly shut the cover of his iPad and sat back. "Just don't let any red flags come up, all right? Stay the course, and we'll plan another check-in soon."

Willow nodded and stood. "Thank you."

As she turned to leave, Landson spoke again, his tone less official now. "I sense you're carrying a lot on your shoulders, Ms. Mercer."

She paused in the doorway. "I can handle it."

"Maybe." He studied her face. "But you're still young.

Learn from the past, but don't let it dictate your future." He pressed his mouth together briefly. "From someone who knows."

She offered him a brief smile, a dip of her head, and a wave before stepping back into the hall. Five long strides and a right turn, and she was at her mother's room.

Her heart tightened in her chest, grief of this moment palpable. Chance popped into her mind just then. She'd watched him struggle to say what was on his mind this morning, to almost spit it out, then retract it again.

Maybe … it was grief.

She'd learned grief sprouted as a result of all kinds of loss —even dreams.

Despite her concerns, she'd managed to restart her life and maintain her mother's care without too much disruption. She just hoped no one on the ranch would learn that her mother was on parole. How would Ace react to her having a convicted felon in her immediate family?

No, her position at the ranch was more than a job—it had become her lifeline. And, maybe, more to the point, it was starting to feel an awful lot like a home. The kind of home she had never known.

Willow hadn't planned on that twist in her life, but now? She would not allow anything to jeopardize all she had gained.

Not even Chance Sutter and the way he looked at her at times, almost like he could see through her walls. Theirs was a new friendship, an alliance at times, like last night, as they worked to move the guests to safety. She hoped they'd continue to bond, rather than spar in the kitchen.

But sharing her secrets? No. That would be risking far too much.

Willow drew in a deep breath, laid her hand on the door of her mother's room, and paused. Then she said a silent prayer to the God who hears and pushed it open.

Chance leaned his frame against the open doorway, hat pulled down snug and low, arms crossed. From beneath his brim, he surveyed the pale shimmer of sunlight stretching across the pasture that he'd long known, first as a kid coating his bare feet with mud, and, later, as a young man, learning to ride his horse across the land.

Fingerprints of the storm lay everywhere—muddy boot tracks, soaked hay, dampened linens still hanging over the side fences. Even the old, ragged posts that held up the barn had yet to dry clear through.

He pushed off the wall with his boot. Maybe he'd change a thing or two about that storm, but when the air smelled like it had just been laundered by spring, he couldn't help but appreciate what was left behind. He walked around back, reliving memories of growing up here, where late-night shenanigans with his brothers were tradition.

After his little stop at the beach this morning, he'd come back, stuck his boots back on, and had been working ever since. He and some of the hands finished hauling away trash from last night's adventure. Rafael threw out a *Good Mornin'* in passing, but otherwise, he'd been AWOL.

Fine with him.

Chance hauled a barrel full of feed around to the other side of the barn, and as he did, his gaze drifted to the small cottage where Willow lived. He could tell she'd come back to the kitchen briefly after their encounter at the beach this morning, but she had disappeared soon after tidying up after the guests had finally rousted, downed coffee, and left in a hurry.

She had not offered him an explanation of her whereabouts, and his father had made it clear he had no jurisdiction over the main house staff. Though he told himself it was none of his business, a knot formed in Chance's gut as he tried to guess where she might've gone.

Could've been a doctor's appointment she was headed to.

Or maybe … breakfast with a boyfriend at one of those fancy little places in downtown Topa Springs.

His stomach clenched, and he scowled. *None of my business.*

He plunked the barrel into a patch of weeds, rays from the overhead sun dusting him on the chin. Puddles that mirrored the sky were mostly dry now, and a slight breeze stirred up broken daisies, scattering them across the grounds.

His ears perked. Tires crunched along hard earth. Willow pulled up to her cabin in that sorry car of hers, and slowly stepped out, her shoulders slumping forward. On her way up the path, she stopped, and shading her eyes, turned toward the barn.

He swallowed involuntarily. She was … lovely. Graceful. He tried to look away, and when he could not, he found himself noting the way her gaze skimmed the ranch, as if assessing the damage left behind by the storm.

That's it. Keep it business. All business.

She stopped moving when their eyes met.

Chance doffed his hat. "Hey," he offered. It had been the second time he'd greeted her that way today. He might be getting used to it.

She reacted with a slow smile, turned fully, and took steps toward him. "Didn't see you there at first."

"I've been keeping an eye out for you."

This seemed to startle her, and one eyebrow rose. "You have?"

He shrugged. *Way to play it casual.* "You disappeared after the beach."

"Oh. Well, I had an appointment." She cinched her purse over her shoulder, holding it close to her body. Almost protectively. "Don't worry. Ace knew I wouldn't be here."

Reflexively, Chance's jaw clenched.

Willow shrugged, a smile appearing on her face, though it looked forced. "It's a standing appointment. Not a big deal."

"If you say so."

Her eyes clouded over, as if holding back another kind of storm. Maybe he should've minded his own business. Remorse at his flippancy twisted in his gut. He reached forward, his hand landing on her forearm.

"You okay?"

She nodded yes, but her eyes continued to hold something darker.

He didn't push. But he didn't walk away either.

"Sure?" he asked softly.

She exhaled, a shudder flowing from her. "I went to visit my mom. She's in a care facility nearby."

He blinked.

"I've never really mentioned it to anybody, so please—"

Chance straightened, chagrined at his nosiness. Clearly, this was a private matter. "It's your business. I'm sorry she's not well, but it's not my place to pry. You don't have to tell me a thing more, you know."

She didn't move, didn't attempt to get away. Instead,

Willow contemplated him, shadowy questions playing across her face. Quiet stretched between them, the afternoon raining down light. In the distance, a hawk called out, faint and melancholy.

"She's been there a while," Willow said, finally. "They think she has dementia. That part's, um, pretty new."

Chance shifted, a memory blazing through his mind. "That's rough."

Willow lowered her gaze. She drew circles in the hard dirt with the toe of her sneaker. There was resignation in her voice. "Life wasn't easy for her even before she got sick, but now"—She shook her head—"sometimes it feels rather impossible."

"Does she recognize you?"

"You know, yes, she usually does. Not always my name, but she trusts me."

"That's something."

"Right now, it's everything."

The weariness in her voice sounded familiar. It went deeper than fatigue. It was the kind that came from watching someone you love slip away one day at a time.

Like the kind he had avoided. He bit the inside of his cheek and attempted to brush away lingering guilt.

"It's okay." Willow turned her gaze to the pasture, where fresh green shoots of grass had begun their stretch upward. She made the move so abruptly that it almost felt like she'd done it on purpose.

Maybe she didn't like talking about the hard things. Like mothers who were sick.

He trained his eyes on that pasture, too, rather than let them land on her face, where his gaze would likely stay. "After my mom died," he finally said, "I used to come out here." He pointed. "Right out to that fence line. I'd sit there over on that top rail, waiting."

She kept quiet a beat, then softly asked, "What were you waiting for, Chance?"

"I was waiting for her voice to come back to me."

Willow turned, surprised.

"She could be so loud." He laughed when he said it, though it still hurt. Sang while she worked. Always humming. I didn't take it too well when her sickness took a turn. Took off for school, believing if I weren't here to see all the pain, then it never happened."

"We all do that sometimes. Avoid the hard things."

"Yeah, well, I said I would come back home, but"—he shrugged—"she passed before I ever did."

His voice dropped. "I think that's why I get so twisted up around Ace. Then again, he forgave Rafael like it cost him nothing. Like that kind of grace was easy. But when I left— when Mom got sick—he didn't say a word. Not 'go chase your dreams.' Not 'stay.' Just silence."

"And you've been carrying that silence like a verdict ever since."

I abandoned her when she needed me." *When Ace needed him.*

Willow's face softened. "You never meant to leave her behind or make her feel abandoned. I bet if you told all this to Ace, he would say the same thing."

"Selfishness isn't usually planned." He pressed a hand against the throb in his neck, guilt rising like tidewater. "I failed her. Ace knows it. I know it."

"Chance …"

"That sound in your voice sounds an awful lot like pity." He shrugged. "Listen, I've made my peace with myself."

"Have you?"

He nodded decisively. "Yes. My memory of my mother makes me, well, it makes me want to do better with this life I've been given."

She watched him quietly, her eyes unwavering. He no longer cared to have the attention on him and what he should or should not have done in his past. Right now, he cared much more about the sadness filling her eyes.

"Tell me about *your* Mom," he said. "Is she safe where she is? Do you have any qualms about her staying there?"

She hesitated to answer him, her eyes darting off toward the distance. Then she returned his gaze and nodded. "Sorry I disappeared there. It's just, well, yes, the staff is good to her. She even has a garden view, which I like."

"I'm sure that helps."

"It does." She waved her hand in a sweeping motion. "Something about God's glory all around does the heart good."

He caught himself smiling until her expression faltered like a one-two punch to his gut. Something was coiled up tight beneath the surface. He'd noticed it in her cadence when she exited her car, and now again, as she mustered up a smile only to let it fade away with her words.

"You're not alone, you know," he blurted. "Even if it feels like it sometimes." He immediately regretted his words. Wasn't his place to comment on something so … personal.

Was it?

Willow looked away, blinking fast. "Sometimes I forget what that even means."

Instinctively, Chance reached out, his fingers brushing her elbow, before he pulled them back. "I mean it." His resolve to be honest, to be in the moment more often, was growing.

She said nothing, but the creases in her forehead relaxed some. So did her shoulders. A rush of a breeze sent a rustle through the trees.

Willow lifted her chin, a suspicious smile curling her lips. She shaded her eyes with her hand. "Why are you being so kind to me all of a sudden, cowboy?"

A woosh of a sigh escaped him.

He tried to think of something light-hearted to volley back to her, but instead, all he could think of was the truth. "Because I know what it's like to lose something slowly. Wouldn't wish it on anyone."

Her eyes glistened now. "Yeah." She turned her gaze toward the small cabin she called home, the same one Patsy did while in residence at the ranch.

Quietly, he asked, "Can I walk you back?"

"You may."

They began to walk in unhurried steps toward the cabin, his mind turning over what he had said to her about losing something slowly. Chance slid a glance at her, her face unreadable.

"Something on your mind?" he asked.

"Yeah."

He chuckled. "Wanna tell me what it is?"

"It's that, well, I didn't expect you," she said.

"Expect me to … what?"

She slowed her steps, and turned a wide-eyed expression on him. "To listen."

Chance let that settle between them. Light danced across her face exposing her in a new way.

"Ouch."

Tears sprang to her eyes. "It was supposed to be a compliment. I-I'm sorry it didn't come out that way."

His arm found her shoulders, and he shushed her gently. "And I was attempting to tease you. I'm the one who's sorry."

Willow lifted her gaze to his, relief flooding her face. The dullness in her eyes began to ebb away, until light began to dawn in them. "I think I'll go inside and rest before it's time to make supper," she said, without any bitterness.

Reluctantly, he pulled his hand from her shoulder and nodded after her as she slipped inside, a tiny smile of acknowledgment on her face.

She'd given him a glimpse. A glimpse of herself that he hadn't known that he needed. And, in this moment, it was enough.

Chapter Six

The next morning, Willow leaned against the farmhouse sink, whipping a whisk around in a metal bowl. She hummed softly, the song something her mother used to sing. No doubt spending time with her mom yesterday had unearthed more memories.

A clean breeze poured in through the window, carrying a hint of moisture with it, though she'd not heard of any rain coming. She glanced outside to find nothing but blue sky and sporadic white clouds.

She set the bowl on the counter and breathed in the herby scent of lemon sage planted beneath the window.

Rising at dawn had allowed her to move through the satisfying motions of meal prep—breakfast, lunch, and supper too—without the pressure of rushing. Not to mention the clomping of boots through her freshly mopped kitchen.

For once, she wasn't anxious at the thought of having her kitchen infiltrated by hungry ranch hands covered in the day's soil. (Though she'd still point them straight toward the washroom sink before they'd get even one bite to eat from her!)

That quake-and-storm combo that had attempted to upend her hard work the other night must have swept away more than just linens and table settings —it had shifted something in her too.

Or maybe it was something else. Her drive to the beach? Chance's heartfelt confession? Or maybe … the gentleness in his voice when he spoke about his mother and assured her she wasn't alone.

His kindness was unexpected. And it meant the world to her.

The soft padding of rubber sandals across the vast tile floors brought her mind to the present.

"Mmm … blueberry cobbler?" Bella's sunny voice lit up the room. "And is that 'Great is Thy Faithfulness' I hear?"

Willow smiled. "Good nose—and ears too!" She tapped the metal bowl on the counter. "Made some fresh whipped cream to top off the cobbler when it's ready."

"Church and dessert! Is there anything better?

"Not in my mind."

Bella dumped a bundle of fresh arugula, curly kale, and golden beets with the dirt still clinging to their roots onto the counter. "This harvest is from our place down the hill. There wasn't a lot left when we moved out, but I brought the leftover to the cabin. Thought you might like some too."

Willow wiped her hands on her apron, the one that said *An apron is just a cape on backwards*, and crossed the kitchen. "Fantastic. I can add it to some quinoa and maybe make a warm salad tonight." She reached for the veggies. "Thank you so much."

"No, thank *you*. You're really an angel," Bella said,

perching on a stool at the counter. "My sisters eat pretty healthy, but, I don't know, sometimes they think I eat too many vegetables."

"As if that were even possible!"

"Right?" Bella laughed.

"Well," Willow said, plopping the greens into an old-style metal colander, "I like food that makes people feel nourished. Don't tell the guys, but I chop up veggies and hide them in their burgers."

"Mum's the word." Bella laughed again. "You're so good at this."

"At what?"

Bella leaned her head to the side. "All of *this*. I enjoy cooking, but managing a kitchen is an art. You do it really, really well."

Willow felt the compliment come in for a soft landing, and she was taken aback. Other than Kit, who popped in occasionally but otherwise made herself scarce, she wasn't used to hanging around other women at the ranch. If life were different, if she weren't so tied to work and looking after her mother's affairs, Bella was the type of person she could laugh with over coffee or join on a long walk through town.

Bella surveyed the kitchen, eyes lingering on the open shelves stacked with colorful plates of varying sizes, and the wide, wooden counter, scrubbed clean but scarred from use. "It's gritty here. Real and homey. Does that make sense?"

"Yeah, I think it does." She leaned long arms onto the counter, her hands clasped together. "Patsy said that the place should feel like someone's mama cooks here, and I've done my best to follow her lead."

Bella smiled, continuing to take in the entire breadth of

the room. Her gaze drifted to a corner cupboard, its glass cabinet filled to nearly overflowing. "What's in there?"

"That's where Ace's wife, Mae, kept kitchen notes. Some cookbooks too. Patsy said she used to refer to them sometimes, but, honestly, I haven't had the nerve to dig through it all. I brought my own with me when I moved, mostly recipes my mother made."

Bella slid off the stool. She stood in front of the cabinet where the handwritten recipes were stored, many on yellowed envelopes and index cards. She turned back toward Willow. "Do you mind?"

"Be my guest."

Bella opened the old cabinet gently, almost reverently. Willow stepped up beside her.

"So many …" Bella said.

"Yeah …"

Bella quirked a smile at Willow. "Wanna take the top shelf while I sort through the bottom?"

Willow shrugged. "Why not?" She put aside her agenda for the time being and began digging through the creaky vintage cabinet. She plucked a cookbook from the shelf, and several loose pages, hardened from spills, slipped out. Her hand landed on a small, leather-bound notebook that looked more personal than the store-bought recipe books on the shelf.

"This looks interesting," Willow said, opening it up. The crackle of pages stiff from lack of use filled the quiet kitchen.

Bella looked over her shoulder. "What's that tab say? Olive … oil."

The pages were filled with tidy cursive, the way her mother still wrote today. Inside were pages of notes and doodles of tree branches. "Seems like she was interested in cooking with olive oil more, maybe?

Bella pointed to the corner of one page. "Someday … from our very own grove." She paused. "Oh. I think she wanted to grow the olives!"

Willow sucked in a breath. "Wow, look at these notes about … about varietals that could grow in these coastal mountains. Oh, and these are some pressing techniques."

"How sweet. She had plans," Bella said, her voice a whisper. "Can you imagine the ranch being a place to grow olives? Sutter EVOO!"

"I'm not so sure what she meant here. Maybe … wait!" Willow looked up. "The tree stand out beyond your cabin, Bella. I think—I think those might be olive trees. No one has ever said, though."

They both paused, quietly thinking.

"Maybe they're just dormant," Bella said. "I could ask Rafael about them. Not sure if he'd know."

"In the meantime, I'll see what the internet can tell me." Willow sighed. "I'm super interested in finding out the possibilities with those trees."

"Gosh, it would be fun to find out if they're still viable."

Willow nodded. "Agreed." She ran the pads of her fingers over a page of notes. "Feels like something rather special, I'd say. I feel, I don't know, protective of her plans somehow."

"Reverent." Bella paused. "You know, some people use oil for anointing, like, for healing. The Bible says it was used for consecrating priests and such."

"Hmm, yes. I recall that too. It's a symbol of joy and blessings." Willow tilted a look at Bella. "Maybe that's what drew Mae toward wanting to grow it."

Willow sighed. "Would be so nice to revive her dream, wouldn't it?

Bella slid a look at her. "You think Ace would let us try?"

"Well, he's really a softie once you push past his gruff exterior." Willow caught eyes with Bella. "You didn't hear me say that."

"No, I did not."

"Chance gets his gruffness from his father, I think." She paused. "That's something else you didn't hear."

Bella laughed lightly, then turned earnest. "Funny you would say all that—not that I heard you or anything. But, *seriously*, I overheard Chance and Rafael out in the barn earlier. Sounded a little tense."

Willow shut her eyes, swallowing back any kind of response. She laid the notebook on the counter.

"It wasn't like they were in a full argument or anything," Bella added quickly. "But, I don't know, there was something testy about it, like when two strong-willed people are on a road trip and each one is sure that their route is the absolutely best one to take."

Willow bit her lip. The oven timer let out a *ding*, offering her a chance to regroup her thoughts. She put on two mitts and opened the oven door, the sweet aroma of warm blueberries filling the room.

"Oh, gosh, you're not saying anything," Bella said. "Guess I overstepped. It's just, I know we're new around here, but Rafael's trying, I know he is. We don't want to cause any trou—"

"You're doing no such thing." Willow set the cobbler onto the counter next to the notebook. Slowly, she took off the oven mitts. "They'll work it out. Don't worry."

"Do you think Chance would rather we not be here? I've asked my husband, but all he does is shrug."

Willow felt the heaviness of Bella's question in her chest. She was beginning to learn that Chance had struggles that he clearly hadn't wrestled into submission yet. He hadn't said anything to her about Bella, but she'd noted the tension whenever Rafael was around.

Her mind scuttered back to that conversation she'd accidentally heard part of at breakfast one morning. Ace had just announced that Rafael would be taking Sparky's spot as foreman. She had not been privy to the entire conversation, but she'd sensed that the father-son conversation was less than pleasant.

She didn't want to mention anything that might betray Chance, but she'd let him know already, in her own way, that she hoped he'd give Rafael a chance to prove himself.

Finally, she said, "What I know is that it's been a long time since that cabin has looked so loved. Sparky was, frankly, a dude who took his boots off there and that's about it!" She laughed. "But you … you've refurbished the garden already and filled the place with the pitter-patter of sweet little paws. What in the world is not to love about all that?"

"Right?" Bella put her hands to her heart, her expression grateful. Just when Willow thought she was off the hook, she added, "So you're saying he's not hostile, just … prickly?"

Willow let out a half-laugh. "Um, I'd say cautious. Yes, that's a good word that won't get me into any trouble."

"Ha!"

"Shush!" Willow leaned forward, her voice a whisper. Her eyes snapped toward the gooey dessert. "Wanna try it?"

"What sort of question is that?"

Willow clucked a laugh, grabbed some plates, and dished

up two scoops of the luscious dessert, topping it off with homemade whipped cream.

"Mmm." Bella savored a bite. "So decadent, but honestly, pretty healthy, if you ask me."

"That's what I was going for—decadent and healthy."

"Getting back to Chance," Bella said.

Willow gave her a *must we* look.

"Why don't we give him a little project to help us with, you know, something to channel all that extra energy into."

Willow caught the spark in her voice. "The olive trees?"

"We could go over to that barn and present a united front. Just an idea. We could bat our eyes and—"

"Oh, no-no-no, I'm not batting anything." Willow pushed away from the counter. "I'm just the help around here."

"Sure, you are."

"Stop it. Anyway, you want to interrupt two hard-working cowboys and pitch them a dream from a decades-old notebook?"

"Yes," Bella said without hesitation. "And you're going to help me."

Willow scoffed. She looked out the window, where shoots of green rustled in the breeze as far as her eyes could see. Spending more time out there sounded awfully inviting.

She turned back toward Bella. "Fine." She picked up the notebook and at the last second, grabbed a basket of scones she'd made earlier for the hands. "Let's go plead our case."

They stepped into the sunlit yard, the sky clearer now. Together, they made their way toward the paddocks, not far from where the olive trees stood in full view, not sure what they'd find—or how their idea would be received.

Chance cinched the strap on a saddle, tugged it once more for good measure, and stood. The gelding, calm with a coat of brown splashed with milky white flicked an ear but didn't move.

Rafael borrowed this very horse last year when he was wooing Bella, or so he heard. His cousin had come up here to make his peace with Ace and ended up borrowing two horses to take his love for a ride on the beach.

Unless … maybe that had not been his intention all along. Maybe he wanted something even back then, and making peace with Ace was an afterthought.

"Hmph." Chance rolled a look across the paddock, where Rafael was working with a hand to check latches on the feed bins and gates. He shook his head, a frown growing on his face. The clipboard tucked under Rafael's arm—and the worn-down pencil behind his ear—was a sight.

Honestly, though, as a former accountant who had his own old school ways, Chance didn't really hate it. Wanted to —but didn't.

He wiped away his frown, replacing it with the most blasé look he could muster.

Truth was, Rafael had been trying. Every movement was measured. Over-the-top efficient. Chance knew he should appreciate the man's efforts, but he fought it. He scowled at his pigheadedness, but didn't do a thing to bury the thoughts that kept poking up through the soil of his mind.

It wasn't that he had a thing against efficiency. It's just …

his teeth were on edge watching Rafael step into his new role and life at the ranch. Jealous? Maybe. Probably not.

Felt more like he was upside down. Disoriented. Too many changes had come to the ranch, and yet nothing had changed at all. Still up early with crows, consuming a heaping hot breakfast after the morning chores, and ending the day with the spectacular "pink" moment that flashed against the Topatopa bluffs at dusk, a memorable way to settle everyone down for the evening.

Speaking of changes, Chance had noticed another one just this morning. That frown slipped back onto his face as he sauntered back across the paddock. He cleared his throat.

Rafael tipped a look up.

Chance crossed his arms in front of him. "That a new rotation you're testing?"

The sun caught the edge of Rafael's jaw. He looked out toward the horizon. "Don't know yet. Adjusted the feed timing for some of 'em, giving that a try. Ace wants the colts calmer during training. Less bite."

Chance nodded slowly. "Didn't know he mentioned that."

"Over at the house this morning—he said it then." The words came from Rafael smoothly.

With a brief nod, Chance flicked a glance toward the main house. "Makes sense."

Rafael tapped the brim of his hat backward. "I'll loop you in next time." He paused. "Didn't mean to leave you out."

Chance cringed. First, Ace, now this kid considered him an afterthought to the ranch's plans.

He dug the heel of his boot in the dirt. Or maybe Rafael meant that response as an olive branch. A person didn't do that unless they thought they had offended someone.

"Appreciate you looping me in," he said, his tone flat.

Rafael didn't say a thing. That was almost worse.

He'd barely taken four long steps before a pair of familiar voices reached his ears, one of them, especially, landed like a soothing balm. Willow and Bella wandered to the paddock and leaned over the sides, their arms dangling.

"Hey, boys." A familiar notebook hung from Willow's fingers over the rails. He couldn't remember where he'd seen it before, but knew he had.

"Come have some scones," Bella called. "You need your strength!"

Chance rolled his eyes, but dutifully approached, wiping his hands on his jeans.

"Are we interrupting anything?" Willow called out.

"Not at all." Rafael joined them at the rail. "We were just about finished."

Chance said nothing, but allowed his gaze to rest on Willow, her lips curved in a half-smile that tugged at him somewhere beneath his ribs. The glow in her cheeks did something too.

"We were promised snacks."

Bella laughed. "Of course!" She handed them each a scone wrapped in a napkin. "We come bearing carbs—Willow made 'em."

Willow lifted the notebook. "And some questions, if you don't mind."

"Ah, so there's a catch," Rafael teased.

Chance's curiosity was piqued and Willow continued, watching him. "So, you know the old corner cabinet in the kitchen? We, um, found something … of your mother's."

Chance leaned in, one brow lifted. "Oh?"

"I hope it's okay." She opened the notebook and thumbed over to a specific page, then held it out for him to see. "There are recipes inside, but what caught our attention are these notes Mae wrote about growing olives."

Rafael's brows rose. "Is there something in there about that old grove?" He jerked his chin in the direction of the stand of trees, though they could barely be seen from the paddock.

Chance thought hard. He reached for the notebook. "May I?"

Willow handed it to him. He began turning the pages, running his forefinger down the faded handwriting. A faint smile played on his face, and he could hardly contain it. "I remember her talking about all this ..."

Willow curled a look up at him, her lashes framing dark eyes. "Do you think those trees could be coaxed back to health?" She was standing so close he could draw in the scent of berries and lavender from her.

Bella was watching him closely.

Chance closed the notebook. Vaguely, he remembered that his mother would keep it—or one like it—open on the kitchen island, jotting ideas into it whenever the wind blew one in.

That same glimmer that his mother's eyes held—hope, mischief, purpose—emanated from their eyes too. He hated to be the one to break hard news.

"The trees are standing, but they're in rough shape. Ace hasn't had the heart to yank them out."

Willow tilted her head, shielding her eyes with her hand. "She wrote about the grove like it was something beautiful. Like she had a plan."

"She did," Chance said softly. "Mom used to walk the rows every spring since they were saplings. Said the trees talked—if you listened long enough."

Bella smiled, but it faded quickly. "It's been a while since anyone walked them, hasn't it?"

Rafael rubbed the back of his neck. "Ace mentioned her vision once. Said he couldn't keep it going without her."

"And now?" Willow asked, gently.

"I'm game to look into it." Rafael lifted a look at Chance. "But it'd take effort. Some money too. Soil testing. Clearing. Irrigation checks. Things like that."

"We're not saying today," Bella said quickly. "Just, well, something that Willow and I could research together?"

Chance glanced toward the pasture, where mist still curled off the low hills. His mother's grove sat just ahead of that rise.

"You think they'd flourish again?" Willow asked.

"Maybe." Chance met and held her gaze. "If someone gave them some TLC."

Silence settled again, like dust after a long ride. He didn't need to say any more. He couldn't stop them from shining a spotlight on his mother's old plans, even if he tried.

Rafael must have sensed it too. He slapped the rail and stepped back, gesturing toward the horses.

"Well," he said, "if you two are dreaming up olive oil empires, I suppose we better keep the livestock in line. Can't have a stampede ruining your first harvest."

Bella laughed. "No, you cannot!" She handed the basket to Willow.

Rafael leaned toward his bride. "Small dreams first." He winked. "The bigger ones'll come."

As they wandered off, Willow bumped Chance's shoulder lightly with hers. "Is this really okay with you? To, at least, check them out? Would be amazing if they were viable. Just think of what we could do—and what food I could make for you all!"

"Don't mind the asking."

She turned an inquisitive gaze on him. "But?"

He lifted his chin, squinting into the noonday sun. "Sometimes I mind the remembering."

Willow sighed, a small nod of agreement. "That's fair."

After a beat of quiet, Chance glanced at the basket. "I don't suppose you could spare another one of those." His mouth was already watering at the thought of the sugar-dusted bread.

Willow handed him a scone, arching a brow as he took it.

"Wait," he said, holding it up for inspection. "You made this one, right?"

"Is that a problem?"

"Only if it's hiding another raw center. I'm still in recovery."

She rolled her eyes, but a smile tugged at her lips.

He took a bite anyway, chewed, then gave her a solemn look. "Worth the risk."

Willow shook her head, laughing now, and the sound of it settled deep in his chest—warm, familiar, like something he hadn't realized he'd missed until it came back. He watched her a few seconds longer, laughter still lighting her eyes.

Yeah.

He was in trouble, all right.

Willow sat cross-legged on a woven blanket just outside

Bella's garden fence, an iPad open and balanced on her lap, the notes app already filled with snippets of her findings.

They'd just returned from wandering between rows of olive trees, touching the bark and silvery leaves, and taking photos with their phones. Many of the trees showed signs of new growth, though not all had.

Seabiscuit yawned. Bella lay next to her pup, elbows propped, flipping through the pages of an old botanical reference book she had found in a shop downtown.

"Says we should have no trouble getting them to produce again." Willow tapped her screen and held it out for Bella to see. "Olive trees like these thrive in full sun and well-drained soil. It's probably why they're all still standing."

"So amazing."

"Most of these appear to be Arbequina," Willow said, "which are pretty typical in the warmer parts of California."

Bella rolled onto her side and pointed at a sketch in her book. "Some of the trees look like these with their smaller leaves. I read that they are very hardy and could survive a frost.

"Yes, those are Koroneiki trees," Willow said. "Someone must've brought a planting over from Greece."

"Greece!"

Willow laughed. "Hate to break it to you, but most of the olive trees out here were brought from places like Greece, Italy, and Spain. Someone even brought cuttings from France."

"Wow." Bella rolled over onto her back, shading her eyes as she looked toward the sky. Seabiscuit padded over to inspect. After giving Bella an indignant sniff, he plopped back down and went to sleep.

"Here, I think I've identified this last one." Willow tapped to flip a page of her iPad. "Arbosana. It's slower to mature but produces sweeter olives. I think Mae chose these on purpose."

"Because they complement each other so well."

"Exactly."

Bella whistled low. "How did we ever get so lucky, Willy?"

"I've been called a lot of things, but Willy's a new one." She gave Bella a pointed look.

"I like it."

"Okay—Belly."

Bella curled her lip. "Fine! I'll come up with another nickname for you."

Willow laughed. "You do that. Now, from what I can tell, these trees have been dormant a long, long time."

"Except for those two in the middle that have some olives on them right now."

"Right. Anyway, Patsy never even mentioned anything about them to me."

"Sounds like no one really knew what to do with them once Mae was gone." She gave a sad little sigh. "They were forgotten."

"But still rooted," Willow said. She could relate to that, in some ways. Life as she once knew it felt long gone. Still, she had a sense of grounding, a deep hope that, despite the gum and pins that held her situation together, it could all work out. Her mother would be safe in her new home, her disease would slow, and her uncle would continue to stay far, far away.

"Hel-lo?"

She snapped her chin toward Bella, whose eyes were closed against the honey-yellow warmth of the sun. "I haven't gone anywhere."

Bella turned over and propped herself up on her forearms. "If you need to get back to the kitchen, I can help you."

"I have a little more time but thank you for the offer." They had been sitting out here for the better part of an hour. Rafael had offered lawn chairs, but they had opted to sink into the grass and watch the bees buzz around Bella's burgeoning garden.

Between them, a half-empty basket of biscuits lay next to a drained pitcher of iced tea. Willow glanced out to the grove of trees again, seeing them far differently than before. Now when she looked toward the olive grove sloped gently up a hill, the trees dusty with age and stillness, she noticed something brand new.

She saw life.

Willow stared at them now, trying to envision Mae's dream. "They're just waiting for someone to love them."

"Sounds like poetry," Bella said. "Or maybe a Sutter Creek Ranch metaphor."

"Want some bread with that cheesiness?"

Bella giggled.

Willow laughed too, but the metaphor stuck with her. Her own mother had waited for that very thing. She'd made decisions in the name of love, only to have everything she had worked so hard for taken away from her.

And, by extension, it had all been taken away from Willow too.

More than the trees needed tending here—Ace and Chance needed to mend the rift between them. Oh, on the outside, their relationship looked solid, but she'd seen them spar over meals, noticed the tension and dark glances. Theirs was a family that had grown wild at the edges, and if they weren't careful, their fragile foundation might very well become uprooted.

It didn't have to be that way.

Maybe what they needed was some understanding—and trust. Maybe even the revival of an old dream.

"Do you think Ace will be on board with this?" Bella asked, interrupting Willow's thoughts.

"I feel like he would be. Of course, someone has to tell him about it first."

"Do you think Chance will do that?"

Willow nodded. He hadn't explicitly said so, but this was his mother's dream. She knew in her heart that meant something to him. "I do. I really do. He … he loved his mother so much."

Bella twisted a look at her as if waiting for something more.

"I just mean there's this incredible softness about him whenever he talks about his mother."

"Rafael says she was a sweet lady."

"Oh, that's right." Willow nodded. "Sometimes I forget that she was Rafael's aunt."

"Yes. That's part of the problem between the boys."

"Is that what we're calling them now?"

"Better than brats."

Willow tipped her chin toward the overhead sun and laughed. She fell back onto the blanket, weightless and free. Cares didn't exist, neither did stress or worry. Instead, she simply enjoyed the act of *being*.

"Or you'd prefer to call them that," Bella said. "I guess I'll allow it."

This made Willow laugh more.

They lay in the grass for a while, the air pungent with

fresh hay and sun-infused wood. Bella sat straight up. "I think we need a plan."

"Agreed," Willow said, lazily. "I've got to go make supper, but it would be so nice to be pouring our very own oil into our pots and pans. Still …"

"Still?"

Willow sighed. "It's going to take a lot, I think."

"Maybe an irrigation specialist first."

"Yes, and a team for the orchard. Though I think some of the hands might take it on."

"Maybe Ace'll be more open to it if we write up a business plan."

"Business plan? I was just thinking of having Sutter Creek oil around for dipping crusty bread into."

"Oh … so good! But … I used to work in a library and helped all kinds of people draw up plans. Maybe it'll help us pitch it to Ace."

"Correction. It'll help Chance pitch it." Willow pulled herself up, tucking her legs beneath her. "I think you're right, though. We should start by researching what we have here, like we're doing now. Then maybe some soil testing, as Rafael mentioned."

"I could sketch out a restoration timeline, since you're so busy."

"You wouldn't mind?"

"Not at all! These baby steps will help everyone get on board. And I'll feel like I belong around here."

Willow quirked a look at her. "Why don't you feel like you belong?"

"Don't take offense. I didn't mean anything by it."

"But something is making you feel that way. Can I help?"

"Well, for one thing, Rafael and I are still newlyweds.

We've not yet had much chance to build a home together, and, though I know he's trying real hard to make everyone happy"—she shrugged—"I can tell that some parts are heavy on him."

"You mean not having your privacy?"

Bella blushed and shrugged again. "Partially that, yes. But also, he and Ace only made their peace last year."

"Oh, and maybe it didn't stick?"

"No, it did. It did. They're on good terms, but I don't think Chance is really on board yet, kinda like I mentioned earlier." She grew silent a moment. "It's not lost on me that this ranch could have been Rafael's, and he knows that."

"What do you mean? I don't understand."

"Maybe I shouldn't have said anything." She shifted and began petting Seabiscuit.

"Bella?"

Bella exhaled. "The ranch once belonged to Rafael's father, many, many years ago. It's my understanding that Ace took it over to, a, help the family out."

Lightbulbs began going off in Willow's mind. This tension between Chance and Rafael obviously ran much deeper than she could have ever suspected. So many questions came to mind.

Bella put a hand firmly on Willow's arm. "Promise me you won't say anything. I've already said too much!"

"Of course, but it's common knowledge, I'd think. It's probably some history that I should know about, if nothing else but to tamp it down when it rears its head." She paused. "Guess I hadn't been paying close enough attention."

"All I'm saying is I want to feel part of this family, and this land, without becoming a nuisance or stirring up bad blood. Does that make sense?"

Willow gave her a reassuring smile. "You could never be a nuisance. Just put that out of your head right now." She forced herself to stand, realizing the time. "I guess I'd better get back because the meatballs aren't going to form themselves. See you at supper?"

"You're not getting rid of me that easily." Bella stood, then scooped up Seabiscuit into her arms. "I'll head over with you so I can talk your ear off some more about those olive trees."

As they walked back, Bella did most of the talking—about recipes for olive oil infusions, about keeping the grove's revival quiet, and also about what the ranch would look like after breathing life into an old dream.

But Willow's mind kept rolling back to what Bella had let slip about the ranch—that Rafael's father somehow lost the land that his son now works.

Chapter 7

Willow returned to the kitchen, her arms and mind full. She dumped the basket, iPad, and a small jar of soil she and Bella had collected from the grove onto the counter.

Meatballs were waiting to be shaped and baked, so she looped an apron over her head, and tied it around her waist. Skin flushed from the sun, she turned on the faucet and soaped up her hands. As the warm water sluiced over her fingers, she hummed "How Great Thou Art" again, grateful to put her focus on anything but lingering questions.

As she removed ten pounds of grassfed goodness from the fridge, her phone rang. Willow bit her lip. She'd dallied long enough. If she were going to get food in the oven, she had to hurry.

She dried her hands on the front of her apron. Maybe a message from Bella with a sudden idea, or perhaps a call about the dinner rotation.

Instead, Topa Mountain Care Home showed up on the screen.

Her heart dropped. Quickly, she answered.

"Ms. Mercer?"

"Yes?"

"This is Jeannie over at your mother's care home."

Willow tightened her grip on the phone and rolled a look up toward the vaulted ceiling.

"Ooh, it's been a day!" Jeannie said.

Willow slid a cryptic look over her shoulder, making sure she was alone. "Is my mother okay?"

"Ruthie's stable now, but, boy, what a disturbance we had today. Your poor mama was shouting and very confused. It took some time to bring her out of all of that." She lowered her voice conspiratorially. "Dr. Grace says it was an emotional trigger that caused it."

Willow pressed the heel of her hand to her forehead. "What happened?"

"Well, see, a man came by asking for her—"

"What man?"

"Said he was family. If you ask me, the two of them do look kind of similar. Anyway, he said he needed to check on her well-being, but my baloney radar went up. His eyes were shifty, you know?"

Willow closed her eyes. "Tall? Mid-fifties? Rough voice?"

"Yep. Like a washing machine full of pebbles."

"Please tell me you didn't admit him …"

"Well, I was on a break, and one of the other nurses let him in."

"What?!"

"But, but I knew he was not on the approved contact list for your dear mama, and I whisked him right out of there. It sure put him in a snit!"

Willow leaned back against the kitchen counter and hung

her head. *No, no, no, no!* Uncle Ray. How did he find them? And why did he want to, after everything?

The woman's voice turned serious. "Our policy is clear, hon. You're the only authorized family member. We've filed a report with her parole office, and there's a note in your mother's chart, but she was just so upset, you know?" Jeannie sighed loudly, as if she was just as upset about this as her mother must have been. "Dr. Grace called the episode your mother had a memory loop."

"I'm not sure what that is."

"Well, she just kept repeating something about the money, not having the money, not keeping the money, and wouldn't let anyone touch her."

Willow's legs went weak. "Oh."

"She's calm now," the nurse continued, her voice softening, "but the doctor recommends a family visit soon. Can you get here within the next few days?"

"Absolutely." She nodded, still holding her forehead in her hands. "I'll come first thing in the morning."

There was a pause. "Now comes the legal stuff." The woman sighed, the sound of turning pages coming through the phone. She began, as if reading from a script: "You are the patient's legal contact and caregiver. We are contracted to stand in your place for a specified time. If we are presented with ongoing risks we will have to—"

"I'll handle it," Willow interrupted. "That was my mother's brother, and he knows he shouldn't be there. Thank you for not allowing him to stay a minute longer in her room. I-I'm so grateful to you, Jeannie."

"You are so welcome, hon." She lowered her voice. "Are you safe?"

Willow's throat tightened. "Me? Yes, he-he doesn't know where I live." *Hopefully.* "Thank you for calling."

Willow ended the call, her fingers starting to tremble. Her uncle wasn't dangerous, just one very big nuisance. A nuisance who could upend all that she had built.

She set her phone on the counter, the hope she'd felt earlier beginning to ebb away. It wasn't fair.

And yet, why was she surprised? Yes, she had worked hard to keep their location secret—even using a pseudonym for her mother—but how easy was it to hide these days with the internet following everyone around like a coyote after its prey?

Willow leaned against the handle of the fridge, pressing her forehead into the cool stainless steel door. Everything had been carefully planned—her job, her mother's care, her past. Like the baby egg-carrying exercise she'd endured in Home Ec class, their new life had been carefully protected.

Now the eggshell was cracking, and she was about to get a big fat "F" on her nonexistent report card.

She barely heard the boots scraping across the tile but straightened when she recognized their cadence.

Chance entered the kitchen, his gait strong, shirt damp in places, and with far less aggression than in the past. He was either only marginally hungry or minding his manners.

"Could use a jug of your ice-cold lemon ..." He stopped when he saw her. "What's got *you*?"

Willow ran the back of her hand across her eyes. "I'm, uh, just tired."

"That's not tired on your face. It's bad news. Something about the olive trees?"

She shook her head. "No, they're beautiful. I hope Ace

and you are open to"—she wiggled her hand in the air— "to seeing their potential again."

He moved toward her, slower now. "Then what happened?"

She bit her lip. Her mother was *this close* to being freed from parole. Willow could not let anything—anyone—stand in the way of her freedom. She would not have it.

The quiet between them stretched. Chance eyed her but waited for her to gather her thoughts.

"You ever try so hard to keep things together," Willow said finally, her voice barely above a whisper, "but the underpinnings of all you've done start to come loose?"

Chance watched her, brows drawing together, eyes darkening.

She swallowed and cast a look through the window. Wasn't as sunny now. "My uncle showed up at my mother's care facility. He's trouble. Not sure how he found her."

Chance's brows knit together more forcefully now. "Did he cause a ruckus?"

"Yeah. Triggered some kind of episode."

He stepped closer, concern on his face. She sensed he wanted to touch her, probably just to console her, but he resisted. Oh, how she could lean into that touch right now ...

She pulled back slightly, allowing more space between them. "What did he want?"

"Money." She shrugged. "What else?"

"Is your mother wealthy?"

"She has nothing." Her voice broke. "Just her basics."

His jaw flexed, something stirring. "Did he threaten your mother? Or the people there?"

"I don't think so, but he's bad for her." *And us. He's bad for us.* "My mother's memory is compromised, but somewhere in the fog she knows him and she's afraid. The nurse who called said it was obvious that he caused her to get upset."

Chance moved toward her. He rubbed her shoulder gently. "I'm sorry, Willow. What can I do to help?"

She stared down at her hands, sorely wishing she could fold herself into his embrace instead of just standing there with his touch on her upper arm. "No one can help." She lifted her gaze, hoping he didn't see her terror. "I, um, I might have to leave. Just for a little while, in case he shows up again."

"Leave the ranch?"

She blew out a breath. "It's a … mess. They might not allow her to stay, but it's, well, it's complicated."

Chance's gaze searched her face. "Why do I get the feeling there's something you're not telling me?"

His tone, both curious and slightly suspicious, brought a lump to her throat. She didn't want to leave here, not now. *Not ever.* But she'd simply told Ace she needed this job to be closer to her mother, not the circumstances that brought her mother to this care home far from Los Angeles, where she once lived.

If she told Chance the truth, what would he think of her mother? Of … her?

"Willow?"

The steadiness of his voice, the deep thrum of it, unlocked a piece of what she had buried down deep. But what if she told him the truth and Chance threw her out?

"You can tell me, you know."

Why was she keeping this such a secret anyway? Surely, everyone's family had skeletons rattling around in their closets. She suspected the Sutters might even have a few.

She wasn't sure when she'd decided to blurt it out, exactly. It might have been the way he coaxed her with his steady gaze, or the way he leaned in ever so slightly, giving her a heady whiff of both earth and smoke.

Whatever the reason, Willow found herself saying, "My mother was convicted of mortgage fraud."

Chance blinked.

She shifted, a headache dart stabbing at her. "My father passed, and I had no idea how little they saved." She paused, willing away the pain in her head. "My uncle told her about a business venture that could save us all—he was broke too."

Chance nodded for her to continue, but did she want to?

She blew out a breath. "He, uh, bought a bunch of rundown properties, got them really cheap, but then he faked the appraisals and took out large mortgages against them."

Chance's brows dipped.

"My mom was a retired schoolteacher who had taken a part time job for a lender. She got them to fund the loans, even though she questioned her brother's ethics."

He whistled.

"I know." Willow shook her head. "I've gone round and round about this for years, replaying everything."

"Were you …?"

"Involved?" She shook her head. "No. It's just …" She wanted to pull back everything she'd divulged about their situation, but it was too late. Their shame had been exposed.

"It's just what?"

She needled her lip. "The thing is, when Mom seemed to have more to her name than usual, I asked her about it. She told me she'd inherited money from an aunt I'd never even heard of. It was easier to just let myself believe her."

"Sounds like you're being much too hard on yourself."

"Trust me, I'm not. I didn't ask questions because I didn't want the answers."

Chance said nothing.

"The truth came out and my uncle got a hand slap."

"But your mother worked for a lender, so she took the fall."

"Yes, she lost everything, and the judge didn't show any leniency. Sentenced her to *years* in prison for her part in all of it. The only reason for her sentence being reduced now is her illness."

"So the care facility is a kind of halfway house?"

"Something like that." Willow blew out a breath. "My uncle tried to milk whatever he could from the fallout. And when she got sick, he tried to guilt his way back into her life. But I wouldn't let him."

Chance watched her, a certain concern in his expression—and perhaps, a touch of suspicion too.

"I was trying to survive."

He nodded.

Willow's eyes stung, but she held his gaze. "Thing is, I never told your father the whole truth about why I took this job, only that my mother was ill and living nearby."

"He doesn't know?"

She shook her head, remembering the little speech that Ace had given her about how carefully he chose his staff, that, once hired, they were representatives of the ranch family. That Sutter Creek Ranch meant something in these mountains. He'd spoke about it all with such pride. She lowered her gaze to the counter, shaking it back and forth slowly. "I didn't mention to him that she was on parole, that she'd been incarcerated."

Chance was so quiet she could barely hear him breathe. If

only he'd say something, so she'd know what he was thinking. She caught his eyes. "I was just so terrified that my uncle would find us again, but it's no excuse."

"Willow—"

"I figured if I worked hard, stayed on task, did the best job that I could, well, that maybe I could keep that part of my life separate. But life doesn't ever really stay buried, does it?"

"No," Chance said quietly. "It doesn't."

The sun was dropping, shadows making their way in through the window.

Finally, Willow moved. She began wiping the island, needing to keep her hands busy. "I'm very sorry that I dragged your family into all this, Chance. I understand if it's all too much."

All he did was nod. Again.

She paused and lifted a question in her gaze. "I should talk to Ace," she said, searching Chance's face for some sign of … what? Sympathy? "Maybe not tonight, but by tomorrow for sure."

There it was again, that nod. He did it once, then just stood there, contemplating her, until he quietly said, "I wish you would've said something."

Heat rushed into her cheeks, regret over what she could lose crushing her. Not saying something could be just as bad as saying too much. The sin of omission. Tears prickled her eyes. A sniffle escaped her.

And all Chance did was stand there.

Willow dropped the rag she was using to mindlessly wipe down the clean counter. When it was clear that he'd gone mute, had nothing more to add other than to stand there with a disappointed expression on his face, she looked away.

She lifted her gaze again, resigned to her reality, only to

watch the café doors flutter shut. And Chance was nowhere in sight.

By the time Chance entered the horse barn, the sky had deepened and a cool breeze had crept in from the west, likely sent by the sea itself. The air hung thick with animals and hay, dust and sweat.

He should've felt lighter. When he'd waltzed into the kitchen to down a glass of Willow's lemonade, he knew in his heart that he'd shown up there for something altogether different than what he encountered.

Simply, to spend time with her.

It all changed in an instant when she shared her secrets with him. It had cost her something, and in some ways, it had cost him too. His heart thudded dully, quieted only by the crunch of gravel beneath his boots.

The barn door creaked softly in the wind. The horses rustled in their stalls, tails swishing, the woosh of hooves shifting in the straw as a lone figure tossed grains into bins.

Rats. He thought he'd be alone with his thoughts here.

Instead, Rafael was bent forward, working away, too focused and efficient to bother looking up at him. Every day that man surprised him.

A colt nickered and Chance paused, allowing his hand to rest on the animal's forelock and down his nose as it sputtered in reply.

Chance paused there, considering Rafael, his work ethic on display. He hadn't expected this from the kid who showed up years ago drunk, who made his mother cry.

A part of him had hoped to find a crack in his otherwise measured, calm demeanor. Maybe even poke the bear some himself.

Otherwise, he would have to expect that Rafael simply had slid right back into place here at the ranch, while he … still couldn't seem to find his footing.

He lifted his chin. "You ever quit?"

Rafael didn't react. Kept working, though he did tilt a look at him briefly. "Not until I'm done."

Chance huffed out a chuckle. "You're never really done though, right?"

"Wouldn't say that."

A quiet beat passed between them.

"This a new thing with you?" Chance asked. "Rafael Sutter—Mr. Calm, Cool, and Collected?"

A brief grin flickered on Rafael's face. "You always walk in with a chip on your shoulder?" he asked, scooping another shovelful of feed into the bin. "Or do you put it on all special for me?"

Chance eyed him. "Depends on the day."

Rafael tossed the last scoop in and set the bucket aside. He straightened, leaning on the shovel handle. "So what kind of day are we having now?"

Chance reached the stall gate across from Rafael. Jaw tight, he leaned against it. Somewhere near the back of the barn, one of the younger colts let out a sputter, as if to say *lights out, boys. It's time for shut eye.*

Finally, Chance spoke. "The strong work you've been doing has not gone unnoticed."

Rafael's brow lifted. "Thanks."

"Didn't expect to hear that?"

"Not from you."

Chance pursed his lips and nodded. "Fair enough."

"So …?"

Chance continued, "That rotation chart you came up with —the hands are responding well."

Rafael narrowed his eyes. "You been keeping tabs on me?"

"Been watching. Yes."

Rafael studied him a moment. "Say what you came to say."

"I've been working my tail off ever since I returned to the ranch." He looked around, taking in the pale golden light dripping from the cross beams. "Just figured I'd expand my hours more when Sparky left."

Rafael nodded slowly. "I get that."

"It's not like I need a title around here for vanity or anything," Chance added. "It's just … Ace hiring you came as a surprise."

"I'm learning that life is sometimes about timing, not who shows up the most."

The truth of that stung Chance more than he wanted to admit. He swallowed. "You probably don't know this, but I left when Mom got sick. Told myself I had to finish my degree."

He kicked his toe against a stall door. "She said she wanted me to go," he continued, "but I figured out the truth: I just couldn't stand to watch her fade."

Rafael nodded, understanding. "And maybe it wouldn't hurt so much if you weren't there in the end."

"Yeah."

"And?"

Chance stuck his tongue into his cheek. "Hurt like hell."

Rafael leaned his back against a post, eliciting a deep sigh. "Regrets are worthless, you know."

Chance didn't look up. "I regret it every day."

A hush settled over the barn.

"I miss your mom too." Rafael said.

Chance closed his eyes. "From what I hear, you stayed with your mom until the end."

"That was a different kind of hard, brother. The kind that makes you lose your temper and then hate yourself for it." Rafael grimaced. "But it gave me time to say things I hadn't said before."

Chance met his gaze. "You did the hard thing. You stayed."

Rafael shook his head. "Stop. You loved your mom, Chance. No question about it. Sometimes grief makes us run." Grey eyes speared him. "But if we're lucky, it brings us back again."

"Like you came back here."

"Well, I can't say that I planned any grand reunion when I showed up here last year to ask a favor."

Chance raised an eyebrow. "To borrow the horses?"

"Yep."

"Hmm. Like you, I've been trying to pick up where I left off ever since returning."

"Maybe you were never supposed to," Rafael said. "Maybe you were always meant to start fresh."

Chance thought about all the times he'd butted heads with Ace since coming back to the ranch, how he'd wanted to digitize the books and the budget and automate milking and feeding.

His father would have none of it.

"You think I wanted this job?" Rafael said, interrupting his thoughts. "I came back expecting nothing. I wanted to apologize to Ace, maybe see if there was still a place for me somewhere nearby. Instead, he handed me this job and said, 'Get to work.'"

Chance glanced up.

"I didn't ask for his trust," Rafael added. "But I'm trying to earn it."

Didn't ask for trust. Trying to earn it.

The words tumbled around in his gut, hitting closer to his heart than he cared to admit.

You know what I'd like to be called? he'd said to her. *Trusted.*

He'd hoped that he had demonstrated to Ace that he could be trusted. Surely, he had. But had he showed that to Willow too?

Wordlessly, Rafael turned back to his work, and the silence between them stretched again. Maybe the reason Rafael was working so hard all the time was he was still paying his penance for time lost.

Chance inhaled. He took a step backward. "I suppose this ranch has enough dirt for both of us."

Rafael flicked his hat back to catch eyes with his cousin once again. "And enough fence to mend too."

Chance laughed under his breath. "There's some truth right there."

Rafael stepped away from the stall, giving Chance a firm nod as he passed. "See you at supper?"

"Sure thing."

Chance kept moving, glancing up at the barn's rafters and the way dust danced on fading light. He hadn't realized how much he needed to pry open his hands and let someone else in to this exhausting, exasperating … magical place.

And for someone to say there was space for him too.

"Hey, Chance." Kit was walking by in the twilight as he exited, a bag of linens hitched over her shoulder.

He dipped his head. "Kit."

She stopped. "That Willow's pretty special, isn't she?"

He crossed his arms and leaned his frame against the wall of the barn. "Makes a mean supper, if that's what you're hinting at."

She rolled her eyes and adjusted the bag hanging from her shoulder. "Okay, fine. If that's how you want to be."

"How do I want to be, exactly?"

"Shew, Chance." She began to walk backwards toward the cabin where she and Eli lived. "I've known you since we were kids, and I don't mind sayin' it—you need someone to soften those edges. Pretty sure you've found her."

"Night, Kit."

She snapped a winsome smile at him. "'Night, yourself, Chance."

He turned toward the barn doors where the light from the house flickered gently in the distance. Willow would be serving up supper soon to hungry hands and his (sometimes) ornery father. She'd acknowledge him when he strolled in, hanging his hat on a hook, and act like nothing had ever cracked in the shell she had created around herself.

But he'd know.

Maybe, he wasn't the only one carrying more than he let on.

He took a step toward the main house, then stopped. There were things to say, but not tonight. Tonight, he had some hashing out to do. With a quick pivot, Chance headed away from the house, hunger far from his mind.

Chapter 8

Keep moving. Don't look up. You'll be fine.

A day had passed, and Willow had done what she'd been hired to do: cook, cook, and cook some more. She kept her eyes trained on the plate in front of her, then the next plate, and the next, and the next.

As usual this time of evening, the ranch house buzzed with the low thrum of boots, clinking silverware, and the steady high-pitched scrape of wooden chairs against worn floors.

Supper had begun and Willow fussed over the buffet and the ranch hands, spooning heaping scoops of mashed potatoes and ladling warm, savory gravy on top. Eli held court at one end of the table, telling a tall tale followed by an eruption of laughter.

She hadn't seen Chance in more than a day. In past months, she might not have noticed, but now?

His absence stung.

Sleep had eluded her last night, her mind replaying snippets from the past few weeks: frolicking in the old olive grove, her surprise of seeing Chance emerge from the sea, that time his strong arms kept her from falling into the creek bed outside of church, and, of course, the morning she'd caught him making a mess in her kitchen.

Oh, how that devilish grin of his faded as he dug his dirty dishes out of the sink and dutifully added them to the dishwasher …

She released a breath in an attempt to clear her mind. With an empty platter in hand, Willow ducked into the kitchen to retrieve more herbed chicken. She was back there only a minute or two when she noticed a shift in energy, a change in the din from chaotic to controlled.

No doubt, Chance had arrived.

She pushed through the café doors and allowed her gaze to find him moving through the small crowd. Her stomach gave a nervous tug. He nodded to Rafael, who had only arrived a few minutes before, then paused to say something that made Eli chuckle. She snapped her sights back to the buffet table, keeping herself occupied with refilling bowls and shuffling dishes.

No sense dredging back up the awkwardness of the other night, and yet she wondered …

Was he still thinking about what she'd said? Or worse— about what she had hidden from him? And Ace?

Willow surveyed the picked-over buffet table, then smoothed a shaky hand down the front of her apron.

"Any more gravy, Miss Willow?" one of the younger hands called out.

She nodded. "Yes, of course." She slipped back into the kitchen to fetch the gravy, grateful for a quick break. When she returned, Chance had claimed a spot at the end of the table facing her. His gaze met hers, but she looked away.

That queasy feeling from earlier, the one in the very pit of her stomach, raised her anxiety again.

She refilled the gravy tureen, served the last plate, and stepped back into the kitchen with absolutely no appetite of her own. She'd already filled and run the dishwasher earlier, so the soft hiss of it kept her company. Wiping her hands again on her apron, she waited for the buzz from the dining room to erupt and clear out.

With her foot tapping nervously beneath her, she tried not to think of what haunted her from the other night. It wasn't the omission of information itself. Honestly, she hadn't thought it was anyone's business to know her family's situation.

But now what bothered her most was realizing her selfishness. She began putting away unused pans and dishes. How would it look to outsiders that Ace Sutter was employing a woman whose family had disgraced itself so?

Remorse twisted inside of her, followed by the very real possibility that her time at the ranch was fading away. The thought of losing her home, and her new family, made her want to crumble into a bucket of tears right here in this kitchen, but she would not have it! Willow set a platter down onto the counter with a clatter. She inhaled deeply. Since when had she let emotion get to her like this?

The door swung open, and she turned with a start.

"Hey." Chance stepped inside.

She straightened, putting on the most unemotional expression she could. "Need something?"

"Yes."

She waited.

"Your time."

She licked her lips, giving him a perfunctory nod. "The guys'll be done soon, so I only have a minute."

He took a step toward her. "That's a start."

"If you're here to say I should talk to Ace before he hears from someone else—"

He was standing inches from her now. "I'm not."

She rolled a look upward. "I understand that our family's … predicament could bring shame to the ranch."

He was quiet for a second, his gaze watchful, gentle crow's feet stretching out from the corners of his eyes. If he moved any closer he'd have to give her a ring. "Stop that."

He'd hooked her with a gaze, but she looked away, her breathing turning erratic. The rise of tears started but she tamped them down. With a measured voice she said, "I don't know what else you'd have me do, Chance."

"I'd have you look at me."

Something tender in his voice drew her. With stoicism, she allowed her gaze to match his.

Chance ran a hand through his hair, his eyes never straying from hers. "Aw, Willow."

She swallowed. "You don't have to say anything, you know."

"Hear me out." His eyes softened. "I've been thinking about what you told me the other night. What hit me in the gut wasn't that your family has trauma—that's as old as time."

She held her breath.

"It's that you wouldn't trust me with your truth."

She let it out, remembering him saying something at the beach … something about wanting to be trusted.

He continued. "It wasn't my business, of course, but you thought I would react—"

"Exactly the way you did?"

"No. You thought I'd have had you thrown out of here." He shook his head, quirking a questioning look at her. "What kind of monster do you think I am? That my father is?"

She raised her hands like stop signs. "That's not ... I don't think that of either of you."

He placed his palms gently against hers, curling his fingers over hers. "My father's a big boy. You don't have to tell him everything, unless you want to. And I hope that you do, because I know him—he'll want to do whatever he can to help."

"Oh ..."

He squeezed her hands lightly before letting go. "And I do too."

Willow's breath hitched.

His voice was sure. "What's happened with your mother, and your uncle"—he hung his head briefly, rocking it side to side—"that's a heavy load. No sense adding guilt to it too."

"I should have told Ace when I was being interviewed."

"So we could help you."

"I-I couldn't imagine that."

"Why not?"

"I ..." Tears flooded her eyes. The kind that came when relief began to show itself. "I've felt so alone, Chance. Every day I have to make decisions between my job here, which I love, and my mother's care—and her future."

"That's a lot for one person to bear."

She swallowed back her tears. He was being kind, but this was her problem—not his. She'd handle it.

"Let me drive you over to see your mom," he said. "I can take you tomorrow."

She shook her head. "Really. No. That's not necessary, it's only a short drive."

"I want to share some of the burden." He hooked a thumb toward the outside. "We can take ol' Lucille if you'd like."

She let out a bright laugh, surprising herself. "I'd rather not."

He blew out an exaggerated breath. "Was hoping you'd say that. My truck it is."

Willow studied him for a long moment. Inwardly, she smiled. The voices from the dining room were growing distant now, and she wasn't sure if it was because every morsel had disappeared or because this moment had eclipsed everything else.

"I don't know what to say other than … thank you."

"That's more than enough." Chance nodded. He turned to go, but paused. "You're not the only one who's tried to bury the past."

Willow tilted her head. "I'm sorry I didn't trust you, Chance."

He held her gaze for a long beat. "You do now?"

Willow nodded. She did. With everything.

The lines around his eyes softened, and he dipped his chin slightly. "Then we're square."

Willow stood motionless, her palms still warm from his touch, and listened to the echo of his boots retreating from the kitchen.

Four days had flown by.

The visit to her mother's care home had been delayed twice—once when another storm rolled in without bothering to announce itself first. It washed out the main road and toppled a power line that took two days to fix. Then again when Brandy McKenna from the neighboring ranch called in a frazzled panic.

Her branding crew had lost two hands to the flu and another to a thrown shoulder. Weather had stymied their schedule already this year, so they found themselves short on both help and time.

The Sutter Creek crew pitched in, which meant Willow cooked for an extra ten cowboys, creating side dishes from leftover cornbread and meat. While grabbing oil for drizzling and coating pans, her mind wandered to the dream of turning that old orchard into something new again. She also sent up a prayer or two for divine intervention to calm the frenetic pace of those hours.

But calm had come. At ten a.m., Chance pulled up in his truck. She had already cooked, served, and cleaned up, and slammed out a batch of molasses cookies for the staff at the care home. Despite all that, she knew that the real word was yet to come—a visit with her mother to smooth things over with the care home.

She'd been praying a lot lately, and today was no exception.

As Chance pulled onto the main road, rays of sunshine stretched across the top of the Topatopa ridges. In its way, that sun was attempting to coax her out of trepidation. She didn't mind it.

On her lap sat a manila envelope with a photo of her Uncle Ray inside. She had already emailed the image to the care home, but hoped to squelch any future visits from him by giving them a photo they could post for all the staff to see.

"You warm enough?" Chance tapped the heating vent, which blew soft and low.

She nodded, voice small. "I am. Thank you."

He let her be.

The silence between them was easier than it had ever been. But he saw the way her fingers picked at the corner of the folder, and the tension-filled way she held her jaw. Eventually, she sighed.

"I hate this."

"I know."

"Going to visit my mother should be a pleasure, something to look forward to."

"Been praying that for you," Chance said.

She peeled a look over at him. "You have?"

"I doubt that coward'll show his face again, but if he does, I'll be ready for him."

She cast another glance at this knight sitting next to her, flesh and blood who *cared*. Wasn't too used to that.

"They show up once," he continued, "stir things up, then vanish before they can be held accountable. Not this time."

She wrinkled her nose, thinking.

"She just can't get evicted. I've got to keep that from happening."

"You show them you're doing everything you can to keep them informed, that you've notified the authorities too."

She swallowed. "Hope it's enough."

He reached over, his hand rough, warm, gently wrapping around hers. "You're not alone in this anymore, remember?"

She relaxed against the headrest of his truck, a sigh escaping her. "I-I remember."

In the parking lot of the care home, Willow pushed aside her initial reluctance at coming here, realizing how very much she wanted to see her mother.

Unfortunately, she'd allowed her worries about her uncle to put a cloud over her plans. That and the lingering concern over another triggering episode.

Chance parked and turned off the engine. "Can I come in with you?"

In her heart, she knew he'd rather stay and watch for anyone suspicious. "No, but thank you. I'll try not to be too long."

He shook his head. "Stay as long as you'd like. I can handle phone calls from here … or whatever else might come up."

She nodded, clutching the manila envelope until it creased in her grasp. Willow scooped up the basket of cookies from the seat, and hopped down from the truck before Chance could come around and open the door for her. She was on a mission to make sure that her mother knew she was safe—and to assure the care home knew she meant business when it came to her uncle.

Willow climbed the small rise of steps to the front door and stopped. She turned back toward Chance, and tossed him a wave. If her uncle dared to show up, Chance would be ready.

At the front desk, Jeannie greeted her. She wore red glasses and hair pinned in a swirl, the kind that's designed to appears messy but actually looks amazing.

"Hello there," Jeannie said, her smile animated. "I remember those cookies—molasses, right?"

Willow handed her the basket. "You got it."

"Bribes are always welcome," the nurse teased. Her expression grew more serious. "So glad you're here."

"How has she been?"

"Great! Gosh, you wouldn't ever know about the episodes if I hadn't seen them for myself."

That's what she'd heard from the doctor when she called a couple of days ago, but hoped the report had remained the same. Her shoulders lowered, a slight sense of calm rolling through her.

Willow handed over the manila folder. "Before I go see her, I wanted to make sure you had a picture of my uncle to post."

Jeannie's smile faded, but her kindness didn't. "Of course, hon. Let me buzz Margie from admin. She's already in this morning."

Minutes later, Willow sat across from Margie, a supervisor with kind eyes and a nubby fleece cardigan that had a tiny, stitched bumblebee at the shoulder. Margie viewed the photo.

"That's him, alright," Margie said, voice soft. "Thank you for providing the photo and emailing the other one."

"He's—he's harmless, as harmless goes."

"Meaning?"

"He's not violent. Just … lazy."

Margie offered a small smile. "Can I be honest with you?"

"Of course."

"Don't let that guy fool you. He is anything but lazy." She tapped the envelope on her desk like a deck of cards. "It always amazes me when people spend so much time trying to figure out more ways to defraud others. Imagine what they could do with all that energy if they were to put it to positive use."

"Had not thought of it that way."

"Listen, my dear, you did everything right. Some people just want to upend others' lives for the sport of it, but we're in your corner here." She kept her expression kind. "I can't promise that your mother's parole officer won't make a change—"

Willow gasped.

Margie leaned forward. "You're doing your very best for your mother. We will be sure to tell him that."

"And if she has another … episode?"

Margie sighed. "The outbursts are something else entirely. Hopefully, those are gone for good now that we know to keep her brother away from her."

Willow pressed the issue. "But if it were to happen again?"

"You're doing the best thing for your mother." Margie's formerly bright expression had dulled some, the creases near her eyes deepening. "We'll cross that bridge if we ever come to it."

Silence landed between them. Willow stood to leave. "I understand."

Margie's warm smile was back. She flicked a nod toward the door. "Go on now. She's waiting for you."

Willow found her mother seated in the chair by the garden window, humming a hymn she couldn't recall the name of, and wrapped in a fluffy sweater. Sunlight from the east-facing window poured across her face, illuminating her smile.

"Hey, Mama."

Her mother looked up. "You're early."

"Nope. Right on time. And I brought you a treat." Willow held up a cookie she'd pulled from the basket. "Made it for you this morning."

Her mother reached for it with a surprising amount of focus. "This is good, but why don't you make the ones with cinnamon on them anymore?"

"Snickerdoodles?"

"Snicker what?"

Willow laughed. "You don't like those."

"Don't like what?"

"Snickerdoodles. That's why I don't make them anymore for you."

"Oh." She took a bite of the cookie and chewed it slowly. Then, "You should make the ones with cinnamon on them then."

Willow lightly snorted. "Okay, you got it."

"I remember something about you," her mother said.

"What's that?"

"You used to eat those yellow noodles every day. Even during the summertime."

"Who doesn't love a bowl of mac 'n' cheese?"

"I don't think dogs do."

Willow chuckled. "Pretty sure they do."

Her mother thought about that.

"Well, Mom, you'll be happy to know that I have a much more sophisticated palate now."

Her mother leaned forward conspiratorially. "Are you sure?"

"I am. I even made okra last week!" She didn't mention that she had to throw the rest of it away after the hands ignored the dish. Even Brandy at the neighboring ranch raised her brows at the offer of leftovers. (She took them to be neighborly, though.)

Her mother wrinkled her nose. "I wouldn't eat that."

Willow laughed again. *Get in line, mama.* "Tell me about your favorite meal here? What does the chef make?"

She clapped her hands together and listed off several menu items consisting of old-fashioned comfort foods like roast chicken, buttered beans, mashed potatoes and gravy.

"Sounds like you have really good food here. I make all of that for the ranch hands too."

"You do?"

"Yes, and they gobble it up too."

"Oh." Her mother was beaming. "I want to go there sometime."

"To the ranch?"

"Yes. Maybe I could stay overnight."

Willow swallowed back the lump forming in her throat. One place she could never take her mother would be the ranch. Another fun fact she had yet to face: When her mother was released from parole, she'd need to find another place for her to live.

The catch-22 kept her up at nights. She longed for her mother to be free from the constant scrutiny of her parole officer, and yet … she'd yet to save enough for her to live as well as she was now.

The soft whiffle of her mother's snoring gave her some relief from talking more about the future. For the next twenty minutes, Willow sat in a nearby chair, holding her hand as she drifted in and out of sleep. In her moments of wakefulness, her mother's mind appeared sharp, showing little sign of the confusion that had brought her here, nor the trouble brought on by her brother.

It was both hopeful and perplexing. With no sign of waking, Willow stood. Then she bent forward, kissed her mother on her forehead, and whispered a promise to return soon.

Chance hopped out of the truck and came around to open the door for her. "Everything go okay?"

She nodded. "They've all seen his picture, and the authorities have been notified." She climbed inside the cabin and waited for Chance to join her. "Mom surprised me. She was in pretty good shape today, even a little chatty."

"Glad to hear it."

Willow gave a half-smile, trying not to think about the new thought her mother had left her with, not to mention Margie's cryptic warning.

Chance put the truck in reverse, drove past a dusty old sedan parked near the edge of the lot, then eased them back onto the road.

"By the way," he said, "I saw no sign of the guy."

"I'm so glad."

"Anything else happen?"

Willow shrugged slowly. "I mean, just the usual. They told me she's doing well, but if there are more outbursts like the other day ..."

"They think there's a risk of that?"

"There's always a risk, I guess. But they were kind about it. Said she might not be able to stay." Willow turned to him with fresh resolve. "But I will figure it out. Not worried."

Chance eyed her cautiously. "Should I be?"

"Nope."

"Hmm."

"Relax, cowboy. I've made it this far."

His expression turned grim. "I didn't mean to doubt you, Willow. It's just, well, I'm trying to tell you I care."

She licked her lips and quickly turned her gaze back toward the window, watching the blur of trees pass them by.

Her voice fell to a whisper. "Thank you."

After a beat, he broke the silence. "So, you see, I can help with all kinds of things: stubborn hands, broken fences ... fierce women."

Willow barked out a laugh, grateful for the sudden change of mood. "Is that right?"

"I'm a man of many talents."

She snorted. "Oh, brother."

He laughed, one brow lifted. "I'm in your corner, Willow. Snort and all."

This time, her laughter dissolved into giggles that went on and on and on.

The call came at dawn.

Willow had just started slicing potatoes when Kit burst into the kitchen, breathless and pale, phone still clutched in her hand like it might burn right through her skin.

"It's Ace," she gasped. "They've taken him to the hospital. Chest pain. EMTs just left with him."

Willow froze, knife suspended mid-slice. "I haven't heard … what do you mean … did they come here?" She put the knife down, her mind racing.

Kit shook her head. "He was out in the paddock with the guys—"

"He never goes out there."

"I know! But he wanted to see what Rafael was up to, and Eli said they were all up there just talkin' about a couple of massive birds that went by when Ace got ill."

"Oh no."

"He's still breathin' and talkin', in case you were wonderin'."

"Good. Great. I'm so glad."

Kit's chin cranked up and down. "Chance went with him. I don't know what we're supposed to do."

Willow grabbed the towel from her shoulder and wiped her hands. Her pulse began to gallop.

Okay." She steadied herself with a deep breath. "We do what Ace would want. We keep things moving."

Kit stared at her, eyes round. "We?"

"Yes." Willow crossed the kitchen and opened the refrigerator, scanning the shelves. "I have a feeling there's going to be a lot of people popping by for an update, and don't get me started about the men—they can be some of the most nervous eaters you've ever seen."

"Really?"

"Really." Willow's arms were full of dishes of leftovers. She pushed the fridge door shut with her bum. "No way I'm running out of food. We don't want everyone eating powdered donuts and cold beans like this is some kind of summer camp."

"You okay, Willow?" Kit stared at her, head tilted.

"Truthfully, no." She was worried about Ace. About Chance. About holding things together while the doctors did their work.

And so she would cook and clean, rinse, and repeat. It's all she had to offer.

The morning passed in a blur of kitchen noise and shouted updates. As predicted, every time she turned around, someone needed something—more food, more direction, more reassurance. She kept moving, kept doing, anchored by duty (and honestly, a little flour dust too).

By midmorning, the bunkhouse porch was full of ranch hands, milling like confused cattle, hats pulled low and shoulders tight. Rafael had left early that morning for Santa Maria, where he'd be looking at some refurbished pumps and irrigation equipment for the olive grove.

Willow carried a tray of sausage and scrambled eggs across the yard. Who cared that it was midday, and she'd had to break into her backup egg supply?

These men were hungry!

She slowed on approach, surprised to hear Chance's voice. She squinted, as if it would help her hearing.

"You two, check that south fence," he was saying. "Don't wait till it gives out again."

"Yes, sir," Joey, the younger one, called back.

"Eli, those water lines near the east meadow—we still leakin'?"

Eli hollered out an affirmative.

Chance nodded once. "Thought so. Patch 'em up before lunch."

Willow slowed her steps, watching as men listened, nodded, moved. Chance neither raised his voice or barked orders, but with every directive, the hands scattered.

A dry laugh rolled out of him when he reached several hands who'd yet to receive an assignment. "Also, just so we're clear," he was saying, "if we lose another yearling, I'm canceling poker night and banning beef jerky rations for a month."

Scattered chuckles lifted from the group as they dispersed. She caught a hint of a smile on his face, which brought her a semblance of reassurance.

Willow reached the porch and laid the tray of food on an empty table. Their eyes met when Chance turned to grab a bottle of water off the porch rail.

"Can I offer you some lemonade instead?"

He nodded, and she poured him a tall glass, handing it to him. "How's our Ace?"

Chance took a long sip. "Stable. They're keepin' him a few days, runnin' tests."

Willow let out a slow breath. "Thank the Lord."

He nodded, eyes meeting hers over the rim of the glass. For a brief second, she thought she saw something flicker there—worry, maybe. But, if so, he blinked it away fast.

"You've done good," she said softly. "Today."

"Don't go ruining my reputation."

She let the moment sit between them before stepping back. Three of the men were still waiting for a word from him to move into action.

In the chaos, Chance had taken hold of the reins, and the ranch was listening.

That afternoon, with nothing to do but wait, Willow and Bella headed out toward the olive grove with boxes of garden supplies—and snacks, of course. The sun was baking the ground beneath them, and the air swam with the faint hum of bees and tractors working overtime.

"I'm so happy to have the garden as part of our new home," Bella said, making conversation. "Rafael says we might even get an early herb crop."

Willow adjusted her grip on the box. "If anyone can coax basil out of late spring soil, it's you."

They walked on, reaching the grove of olive trees that already showed signs of care, their shimmering leaves shining more and browning less. Willow set her box down beside a half-cleared patch of earth and plunked down beside it.

She opened the flaps and froze. "What. Is. That?" She tamed the shake in her voice.

Bella followed her gaze to a black-feathered bird, the size of a small dog, perched on a low branch, its beady eyes trained on them. It had a big, red head that shone like fire in the bright sun.

"That's no turkey," Willow whispered.

Bella strained to see it. "Are you sure? It looks kind of—feathery."

"It—it's some kind of buzzard." Slowly, she started to rise.

The bird took that moment to let out a long hiss, like steam letting loose from a factory. The ugly, rattling sound filled the air as the bird stretched its wings out like a building, silent threat.

Bella let out a squeal.

Willow grabbed her arm. "Don't move!"

"I'm not moving!"

"Don't flap! They sense flapping!"

The bird tilted its head and let out another hiss. Bella let loose a yelp, and Willow—despite herself—screamed right along with her.

"Oh my gosh," Bella cried. "This is like *Snow White*! You remember that scene? The buzzards circling after the witch falls off the cliff?"

Willow's stomach turned. "Yes! I used to fast-forward that part every time!"

"Me too! They're gross! Why are they always around death?"

"Because they eat *dead things*, Bella!"

Another hiss. Another scream.

And then—

Footsteps. Fast ones. Pounding like hooves on dry earth.

"Willow? Bella?"

Chance crashed through the trees, skidding to a stop in a cloud of dust. His shirt stuck to him, his eyes wild.

"What happened?"

Willow pointed skyward. "Buzzard!"

Bella flailed an arm. "It hissed at us!"

Chance's face registered … something. Maybe relief. Maybe exasperation. He dragged a hand down his face and looked up.

"Oh. That's just Gary."

Willow blinked. *"Excuse me?"*

"He hangs out in the grove. Shows up when the weather's warm."

"You named it?"

"Well, yeah. He's a turkey vulture, and he's harmless."

Bella shook her head. "He hissed. At us."

"He does that." Chance stepped toward the tree and clapped his hands. "Go on, Gary. Get."

The vulture blinked, shifted, and launched itself into the air with a gust of wings that stirred dust and leaves alike. It soared once overhead, then glided out of sight.

Willow let out a breath and bent to steady herself on her knees.

"You okay?" Chance asked.

She stood and swatted at her pants. "Yes. I mean—no. That was horrifying."

Chance looked between the two of them, hands on his hips. "I swear, this is the second time today I've had to sprint across the ranch like my hair was on fire. You ladies trying to give me a heart attack now too?"

"We thought we were being hunted!" Bella said, brushing off her shirt.

"You were standing under a bird," he said. "A bird that eats roadkill. You are *not* roadkill."

Willow gave him a flat look. "Still. He hissed."

Chance cracked a grin, then wiped it away. "Next time just holler 'Bird!' I thought someone fell off a roof."

"Well, we're very sorry for disrupting your cardio routine," Willow said, voice dry.

He huffed. "No apology needed. I suppose I should be expecting it daily now, now that you entrepreneurs will be spending your days out here in the wilds."

"Maybe if your bird wasn't a straight-up villain from a Disney movie …"

He tipped his head. "You mean *Gary?*"

"Stop saying his name like we're supposed to be friends!"

Back at the house, after the boxes were dropped and Bella disappeared toward her cabin, Willow sat on the porch steps, sipping lemonade and rubbing the back of her neck. Chance joined her a few minutes later, the sun dipping low over the barn roofs.

"I'm going to have nightmares," she muttered, cradling her glass. "Buzzards and cliffs and Disney witches."

"You'll be fine," he said. "I hear Gary's not one to hold a grudge."

Willow laughed in spite of herself. "Seriously though, thank you."

"For what? Evicting the neighborhood bird?"

"For running," she said quietly. "For showing up."

He didn't say anything right away. Just leaned forward and rested his elbows on his knees.

Willow watched the light shift across the yard, painting the gravel into a burnished end-of-day bronze. The morning had started with confusion and fear, but somehow, everything had held steady.

Ace showed improvement. The barn still stood. The hands still worked. And Chance Sutter had stepped up and proved—without a word of bragging—that he could carry the weight.

"You did good today," she said again, softer this time.

He glanced sideways at her. "You too. Even with all the hollerin'."

She shrugged. "It's a gift."

They sat there a while longer, sipping lemonade and letting the hush of dusk settle over the ranch.

Tomorrow could bring harder news. Or better. No one could say for sure.

But, for now, the fences held, the grove still stood, and there was strength enough—between them—to face whatever came next.

Chapter 9

Chance stepped into the equipment barn, squinting past rows of old tools, rusting parts, and forgotten intentions. He spotted what he was looking for behind the woodpile, under a sagging tarp.

"Tell me again why we're risking tetanus for this?" Rafael asked, ducking under a low beam.

Chance smirked. He set down two large stainless steel bowls, then wiped his dusty palms on the thighs of his jeans. "Because apparently Bella wants to live out her Tuscan farm fantasies."

"And Willow's already planning labels," Rafael added, chuckling. "Saw her doodling 'Topa Gold' on the back of a grocery list."

"That's what makes it dangerous," Chance said. "Once they start naming things, it's already happening."

They moved a few more crates to get closer, then Chance removed the tarp.

Rafael let out a low whistle. "Wow."

The old, decorative press looked like someone's granddad

had built it as a weekend project. The crank still turned, though it let out a groan loud enough to wake the barn cats.

"Maybe it's all Bella's dreaming, but I kind of remember your mom making oil," Rafael said.

"Yeah." Warmth flooded him. "She loved the idea of using the land for more than cattle and hay. I think she got a few jars out of it when the trees were still young."

"Wonder how it tasted."

Chance directed a look at Rafael. "As I recall, Ace said it tasted like sunshine and shoe polish."

Rafael threw back a laugh. "Sounds like Ace." He loaded the press on a dolly and paused to steady it. "Your mom always was an optimist though."

"That she was."

They rolled it toward the barn door, wheels wheezing and whining the entire way. Outside, the smell of fresh-cut hay hit their senses, and Chance found himself warming to this idea more than he thought he would.

"Mom would have loved this idea," Chance said, quieter now. "To see the grove turn into something."

Rafael went quiet before nodding. "She was one of the few who never looked at me like I was a mistake."

Chance glanced at him, then looked away. "Yeah, well … she had a gift for seeing past what was presented to her."

They wheeled the press to the outside edge of the equipment shed. Rafael wiped sweat from his brow with the back of his glove and leaned his behind against a fence post.

"You know," he said, "I've said it before that I never thought I'd be back here. Especially working alongside you."

Chance didn't answer right away. He was watching the press, thinking of what might've been. He gave his cousin a small shrug. "Never thought you'd want to be back."

"I almost changed my mind," Rafael admitted.

"Why didn't you?"

"Found my humility. Plus, my wife said we were moving to Sutter Creek whether I liked it or not."

Chance barked a laugh. "Bella does have a way of getting what she wants, I've noticed."

"Willow's a willing partner in crime too."

A smile spread across Chance's face.

Rafael cleared his throat. "Honestly, I'm glad she pushed me. This place …" He looked out across the land, to the ranch buildings, then up toward the line of the mountains in the distance. "It's still home. Always was."

A quiet beat sat between them. Cautious and careful—like walking across a rickety bridge for the first time in years.

"Let's see if this thing works," Chance said finally, breaking the silence. He knelt beside the crank, tightening the bolts while Rafael unpacked the sample of olives he'd picked up from a grower on his way back from Santa Maria.

He'd already washed the bucket of deep green and purple olives, fresh and earthy smelling. Might not produce more than a shot glass of oil, but that would be enough.

"You want to crush 'em or turn the crank?" Chance asked.

"I'll crush. I've got more years of rage to work through."

"Fair enough." He stood and stepped back, giving Rafael some space.

Rafael poured the cleaned olives into the grinder and went to work creating a thick paste. Skins and pulp squelched under the pressure, and Chance shrank back at the sound—and the look on Rafael's mug.

"You're enjoying this too much."

"Therapy," Rafael grunted. "Cheaper than a shrink."

They each took a portion and mixed the paste in large stainless steel bowls.

After five minutes, Rafael said, "How long did I say we have to do this?"

"Half hour."

He groaned. "Right."

"And that's only step two, well, three, if you count the washing. Guess we should've gotten the ladies in on this."

"Maybe so, but we didn't even know if this old thing worked."

"True."

Finally, Chance handed Rafael a small mesh filter, which he attached beneath the spout while he slowly turned the crank. Drop by drop, golden liquid trickled into the glass.

"Would you look at that," Rafael said, slowing some.

Chance leaned in. "Looks like engine oil."

Rafael grinned. "Smells better, though."

The stream grew, then tapered. Rafael held the jar up to the light showing off the murky but unmistakable measure of olive oil.

"It works." Rafael sounded like he almost didn't believe it.

Chance took the jar and tilted it, letting the thick amber swirl. "Beautiful."

"But will it be enough to start?"

"Not sure," Chance said. "After a few days of working the arm of that crank, the ladies might open up a Kickstarter for a full mill operation by end of week."

Rafael laughed. "I see hydraulics in the ranch's future."

As if waiting for just the right moment, Bella approached from the path, a straw hat perched on her head. Willow followed, wiping her hands on her apron, face flushed from kitchen heat. A basket swung from the crook of her arm.

Bella beamed. "Ooh, what's going on here?"

"Ladies," Chance said, his voice dripping with mock formality, "we present to you Lucille's more respectable cousin—Olivia, the oil press."

Willow raised an eyebrow. "That thing looks like it belongs in a museum."

"Hey, lots of priceless artifacts in museums," Chance said.

He handed her the jar of oil. She took it and held it up to the light. Then she gave it a swirl followed by a tentative sniff. "Oh, lovely."

"It actually worked!" The tone of Bella's voice rose.

"Sure did," Chance replied. "We've got about two tablespoons of Topa Gold right here."

Willow laughed softly, then handed the jar to Bella. "You did it."

Rafael and Chance exchanged a look.

"Yep," Chance said.

Bella blinked. "And without a fistfight."

"Tastes better that way," Willow said with a wink.

Bella linked her arm through her husband's. "Amazing. The olive grove gets new life, the old press gets use again, and nobody throws any punches."

"A Christmas miracle!" Willow said.

"In the spring!" Bella laughed.

Chance shook his head, taking the jar from her. "Oh, come on now."

Rafael snickered.

Willow was still smiling, eyes on the oil. "This has become a dream I didn't know I had."

Chance looked at the jar, then out toward the grove, its

narrow trunks casting long shadows across the late-day soil. "Then let's see where it goes."

Rafael nodded, his tone more practical. "Might be worth getting someone out here to test the soil. We can ask around about acquiring a commercial press, since this is more of a hobby one."

Willow and Bella exchanged a look—not giddy, not wild-eyed, but grounded. Two women used to measuring hope bit by bit.

"We'll think it through," Bella said, careful but sure. "One step at a time."

Willow tipped her gaze toward Chance. "But if we end up international oil baronesses, I'm not apologizing."

He raised both hands. "Just save me a bottle for the kitchen."

"You got it," Willow said, reaching for the jar of oil in Bella's hand. She looked to Chance. "Mind if I keep this?"

"It's yours."

Willow plunked it into her basket.

"We're off to take a look at the grove and see what trees might need a little TLC," Bella said.

Chance's mind stirred. He wouldn't mind if Willow stayed longer, but, of course, she had a short amount of time to do what was on her mind.

He cleared his throat, keeping his voice low. "Enjoy your-selves, ladies."

As the women moved on, their voices a frenzy of talk about possibilities, Chance crouched beside the press. With his fingers, he tightened a bolt by habit more than need. Rafael wiped his palms on his jeans and passed him a wrench.

After a moment, Chance said, "Looks like this thing's got another season in it."

"Yeah," Rafael said. "Some things don't need replacing—just someone willing to give 'em another go."

Chance nodded, still crouched. But his eyes followed Willow's path until she disappeared from view.

"Yeah," he murmured. "Some things are worth the work."

Two small bottles sat side-by-side like trophies on the windowsill, catching the kitchen's warm light—Topa Gold. Willow loved the sound of it on her tongue.

If only there was enough to cook a meal for everyone.

Only a few of the trees had enough growth to produce something, since most of the grove had gone dormant from lack of water and feeding. But starting small had been the plan anyway, and from the look of things, there was hope.

Chance stood at the sink, sleeves rolled back, scrubbing the press's crank handle with a toothbrush, of all things. A dirty tool sat on the counter next to him.

Willow leaned on the doorframe, her eyes brushing over the slight bend of his neck, the gentle shifting of his muscles as he scrubbed, the line of his jaw. He could be doing this out in the laundry area, but she wasn't complaining.

More and more, Willow enjoyed the simple things. Like watching Chance work.

She noticed other things, too, and not just because they seemed to be working alongside each other—and more—these days. He made her laugh. He brought calm and warmth into her days, even on the most chaotic of them.

He shook water from the handle and reached for a towel. She might have scolded him in the past for that—using a kitchen towel to clean his tools—but she couldn't bear to break up the bliss she'd been feeling.

Instead, she said, "Want me to start boiling water?"

"Sure. If you're looking to make exactly three tablespoons of pasta."

"It'll be the best pasta you've ever tasted."

He laughed. "I agree. It would be a start—and delicious too." He spread out the towel on the counter and laid the handle on it. "Your enthusiasm is contagious."

"Don't blame me," she said lightly. "Blame Bella and her Pinterest board full of Italian olive groves."

"She's determined. I'll give her that." He smiled. "But something tells me you're invested in this at least as much—maybe more."

She eyed him. It's true. From the minute she encountered his mother's deliberate handwriting, her dreams, and plans, she was all in. She was curious and terrified all rolled into one.

Something else terrified her ... the way she felt herself expecting him. Letting him near. Wanting him near.

He'd barely touched her, well, except for saving her from certain death in the old creek. But seriously ... the way he looked at her, the things he said, shoot, the things he *did* for her.

And yet, neither of them had professed their feelings for the other. She was living in Jane Austen's world, just waiting for him to ask her father for her hand.

Only her father was long gone, and, frankly, she wasn't sure where she would be this time next year.

Plus, there was the last little tidbit that she'd failed to confess …

Her phone buzzed on the counter behind her. Once. Twice. Then a third time. Her whole body went still.

Chance glanced toward the sound, one eyebrow raised. "Spam?"

She frowned. "Maybe … wait, no. I'll go take this outside."

He didn't press her as she grabbed the phone and backed toward the door. "I'll, uh … be right back."

Chance nodded, and turned back toward the sink, his attention now on the other tool waiting for a bath.

Willow stepped outside, gravel crunching softly beneath her boots. She moved past the side of the house, toward the meadow where she'd have privacy. Her hands trembled as she brought the phone to her ear.

The voice that answered was as oily as she remembered.

"You finally picked up. Thought you were trying to ghost your dear old uncle."

Her jaw tightened. "You know full well I've been trying to reach you."

"Is that any way to talk to family?"

"You lost your place in our family a long time ago. You're not welcome anymore."

"Don't be so dramatic, dear."

"I need you to stay away from Mom."

"And ignore my only living sibling? Not a chance."

"She has nothing to give you, Uncle. You know that." She glanced over her shoulder. "Neither do I."

"Not so fast. I've heard all about that fancy ranch you're living at, the one with the cowboy. That's a hoot!" He coughed a laugh. "Always knew you'd find someone to support your lifestyle. Never thought it'd be a cowboy, though.

"What do you want with us?"

"I hear you have a new venture too. A whole olive oil operation? My, my, you've been busy!"

Willow's heart pounded. "How do you know about that?"

"Doesn't matter. Anyway, my guess is your new business will help you take care of your mother and make a substantial donation to your favorite uncle."

"I told you. I don't have anything left."

"Don't lie to me, Willow. You had money to buy that shiny convertible, didn't you?"

Lucille.

Her stomach lurched. Had he seen her car? The one everybody made fun of?

"I'm not giving you anything."

"You sure about that?" he said smoothly. "Because if I don't see a little kindness from you in the next week, I might just give a call to the local sheriff. Or maybe your boss. Or that fella with the scruffy smile who seems to think you're just a sweet girl trying to find her place."

Willow closed her eyes, dread curling in her gut. "You leave them out of this."

"Then make it easy. Five grand. That's nothing to a rancher's chef." He snickered. "A small price for peace and quiet."

It wasn't so much the blackmailing that twisted her insides—that was bad enough on its own.

What had her heart pulsating in an unhappy way was the one thing she hadn't told Chance. Or anyone. Her mother had given her money for the car. At the time, it seemed like a gift, one out-of-the-blue, surprising, totally unexpected gift.

It wasn't much, but it was enough. She'd bought "Lucille" without asking her mother one question about where she'd found the money. By the time she'd learned the truth, the title was in her name, and she had not one extra cent to her name.

She hadn't used the funds with any malice, but after all this time, truth did not feel quite like a defense anymore.

Her uncle, likely taking her silence as guilt, hung up.

Willow's heart thudded against her ribs. Her throat tightened until it felt hard to breathe. She couldn't let this ruin things. Not after everything she'd done to rebuild. Not when she was finally starting to feel like she belonged here.

The sound of footsteps startled her. She turned sharply to find Chance walking toward her. He stopped at a fence post and leaned against it.

"You all right?" he asked gently.

Willow pasted on a smile. "Yeah, I'll be right in."

He didn't look convinced, but he nodded anyway. "I'm here if you need to hash something out."

She swallowed. She needed more than hashing, she needed a plan. And she needed the truth to stop following her around like a shadow.

But all she said was, "Okay. Thank you."

Chance lingered, his eyes searching her face. "Maybe you've been doing too much lately. Taking care of all of us. Cooking special meals for Ace."

Willow exhaled, grateful for the change in subject. "Don't worry. I'll crash eventually."

"Promise?"

A faint smile tugged at her lips. "Cross my heart."

He walked closer, just enough that she could see the flicker of concern still resting behind his eyes. He didn't press. That was one of the things she appreciated about Chance. He didn't push too hard against her walls.

"I'm here if you need anything." Chance watched her closely, his voice warm and low.

"Honestly, I think I just need … a change of scenery."

He cocked a brow. "I think I can handle that. Want to run away from the ranch for a few hours?"

"I still have to make supper."

Chance glanced toward his truck, then back at her. "Come on, then. Let's take a drive. I know just the place."

Willow blinked.

He reached for her hand, and she didn't pull it away. "I'll get you back in plenty of time."

She hesitated, still—partly because she hadn't planned on going anywhere, partly because she was afraid if she didn't stick to her routines, everything might fall apart. But when he offered his hand, casual as anything, her feet moved on their own.

"Alright," she said softly. "Lead the way."

Twenty minutes later, they parked on an overlook where eucalyptus trees bent in the breeze and the air tasted faintly of saltwater. Willow pulled her hair into a ponytail, securing it with an elastic band from her pocket. The wind tugged at strands of hair, but she didn't care. The sound of the sea made its way into her bones.

Chance offered her his hand. "C'mon."

They made their way down a sandy trail that fanned out to a marsh dotted with seagrasses.

"You weren't kidding," she said, shading her eyes with her hands. "What a perfect spot."

"I figured we'd earned it," Chance said, flashing a smile. "You've been serving up miracles all week, and I've been elbows deep in crank grease—"

"And don't forget—doting on Ace."

"You're the one doing that. I just go in for my daily flogging."

"Ha!" Willow shouldered him with hers. "Stop that."

He laughed.

They kicked off their boots at the edge of a piece of driftwood, then walked barefoot along the surf. The cool water pooled around them, tickling their ankles as they strolled, the sand pillow soft beneath their feet.

Peaceful was an understatement.

For a long while, they didn't speak. Just walked. Sometimes close enough that their hands brushed, sometimes apart. The wind picked up. A gull screeched overhead. Farther down the beach, the outline of a few surfers bobbed in the water, waiting for one last good wave.

Chance stopped suddenly, looked at the water, then at her. "You mind?"

She followed his gaze and laughed. "Seriously?"

"Never leave home without my board," he said with a shrug. "Truck's got everything."

Willow gestured grandly. "By all means, go commune with the sea."

"Watch closely," he said, jogging back toward the parking lot. "I make it look easy."

A few minutes later, he was paddling into the surf, the setting sun painting his silhouette in glitter. Willow sat on a stretch of dry sand, arms wrapped around her knees, watching as he rode one short, messy wave and wiped out spectacularly. He emerged grinning, hair plastered to his forehead, laughing as if the ocean had told him a joke only he could hear.

He was wild and grounded all at once. The kind of man who could rebuild an ancient olive press in the morning and dance with the tide by dusk.

And make space for her too. She didn't deserve him.

Willow lay back in the sand, her eyes tracing streaks of color in the deepening sky. She imagined a few stars blinking back to her, patiently waiting for their light to shine when the time came.

Her phone buzzed beside her.

Chance came up the path just as she checked it, still dripping seawater, his shirt pulled on halfway, surfboard under one arm. "Told you I'd wipe out."

"I'm impressed. Not necessarily with your form, but your bravery."

He grinned, then frowned when he saw the expression on her face. "Everything alright?"

She tucked the phone away before he could see the screen. "Yes. Nothing urgent."

He studied her for a beat but didn't pry. "Ready to head back?"

Though she hated the idea of leaving this moment behind, she nodded anyway. "Yeah. Let's go."

They had just reached the highway that would take them back to the ranch when Chance's phone rang, the jarring sound sharp against the hum of the road.

He checked the screen, sighed, and answered. "Ace." Pause. His brow furrowed. "Now?" Another pause. "All right. I'll be there in twenty. Thirty tops."

He ended the call and cast a glance at her. "Sorry. He wants to see me tonight."

Willow felt her chest tighten. "Is everything okay?"

"No idea," he said. "The last time he wanted a meeting, it was nothing, really. This could be anything. He doesn't always give context—just orders."

She nodded, her mind already spinning. The weight she was carrying had lifted for a while—forgotten, even. But reality had followed her to the coast.

Chance reached for her hand briefly, giving it a quick squeeze before pulling away. "Thanks for coming with me."

Willow watched the coastline shrink in the rearview mirror. "Thank *you*."

She took another peek of her phone. Every minute with him was borrowed light. Even if she didn't deserve it.

Chance dropped Willow off at her tiny cottage and watched her walk inside. He'd become used to sitting beside her with her hair smelling of salt and ocean, and though he hadn't gone looking for any real attachment in his life, it had found him.

He was sunk.

Chance whistled through the revelation, a grin stuck to his mug. He wandered up to the back porch of the main house and looked up to where Ace kept a small study off of his bedroom. A faint glow filtered through the glass. In this small space, Ace stacked up history: books, papers, maybe even a secret or two.

Inside the main house, the air smelled faintly of pipe

tobacco and old leather, and he frowned. Smoking was off limits for Ace. Had been for a long time. He found his father sitting in his usual spot—an armchair by the fireplace, though no fire burned in the hearth tonight. Just the lamp on the side table casting light across Ace's weathered face.

"You made it," Ace said, his voice raspier than usual.

"I made it." Chance stepped inside, his eyes searching for remnants of his father's cigar. When he didn't find it, nor evidence of a pipe, he asked, "Doing okay tonight?"

Ace frowned and stilled his gaze. He was either annoyed or amused. Maybe a little of both. "Not planning to keel over tonight, if that's what you're asking."

"Twasn't, but alright."

Ace gave out a garbled laugh, then coughed into his fist. "Haven't changed, son. I say what I mean. I didn't say come 'cause I'm dying. I said come 'cause I've got something on my mind."

Chance took a seat on the leather love seat. He leaned forward, intent on what his father had to say. He waited, forearms resting on his thighs, hands clasped. Ace didn't like to be rushed.

"Been thinking." Ace shifted in his seat. "Far too much, I admit. Sitting around this much has made me introspective."

Chance smiled softly. "You're not much for sitting still."

"No. Never was. Neither was your mother." Ace's gaze wandered toward the empty fireplace. "She always said I'd die with my boots on. Maybe she was right."

Chance's chest tightened. "Don't talk like that."

"Dying is a part of life, son—but right now, that's not what I'm thinking about."

"I'm listening."

"I think it's getting close to when I will begin to hand off some of my ranch responsibilities. Maybe I'm not there yet, but, in the meantime, I am trying to make absolutely sure that the *right* people are in the *right* place when the time comes for me to take a step back."

Chance sat straighter. "You thinking of stepping back?"

Ace rocked his head side to side, measuring the words. "I can't do all this forever. Between you and me, I've made a few mistakes trying to."

Chance didn't say anything, but the word *Rafael* hovered in the back of his mind.

Ace lifted his chin, looking downward at his son. "I know what you're thinking."

"Tell me what I'm thinking.

"You were blindsided by my foreman decision."

Chance crossed his arms in front of his body. "Didn't have to be that way, you know. We could've talked it over first, presented a united front with the decision."

"Maybe I should've. In hindsight," Ace admitted. "But I needed to see how you'd handle it. Whether you'd get bitter and withdraw or keep showing up."

"And?"

Ace nodded deliberately, his lips pressed together. "You're here."

"Want to know why?" He didn't wait for an answer. "Because this place matters to me—you matter to me."

Ace leaned his head against his chair, his hands folded over his stomach. "You've always done your work. You're reliable. But for a long time, I couldn't tell if you wanted to be here, or if you were just here 'cause there wasn't somewhere else to be."

Chance let out a slow breath. "I chose this. I came back."

Ace nodded, quiet for a moment. "It has not gone unnoticed."

The room was still, the only sound the ticking of the grandfather clock down the hall.

"I wanted you to know," Ace continued, voice softer now, "that when I think about this ranch—its future—I think of you. Not Rafael. Not your two brothers either. They've chosen lives far off from here."

Chance's heart kicked hard against his chest.

"I have more to say on what I've observed," Ace said. "I see how you handle people. How you lead when no one's looking. That means more to me than anything you could tell me to my face."

Chance swallowed against the sudden tightness in his throat.

"You've grown into a man your mama would be proud of." Ace looked him square in the eyes. "And she'd be proud to see you take the reins from me."

"You're talking like you're leaving."

"I'm talking like a realist who is being smart with however much time the good Lord gives me."

Chance tamped down the rise of emotion in his chest. "You've got plenty of time."

Ace smiled, and there was something in his expression— calm, knowing, maybe even peace. "That's not up to me. But what *is* up to me is making sure I don't leave things unsaid."

The quiet that followed was heavy, but not uncomfortable.

"And another thing," Ace added after a pause. "Willow."

Chance snapped up his gaze to meet his father's.

"You think I haven't noticed?"

Chance rubbed the back of his neck. "Yeah … it's complicated."

"What's so complicated about falling in love?" Ace said with a small chuckle. "I've seen the way you look at her. And how she looks at you when she thinks no one's watching."

Chance didn't respond, but he felt every word of that.

"She's good for you," Ace said simply. "Softens your edges. Grounds you. Reminds you to smile every now and again. Your mother did that for me too."

"She's … well, there's things I'm still trying to figure out."

"You never will," Ace said with that deep chuckle. "It's not worth trying because just when you think you've got her all figured out, she'll—"

"Turn on me?"

Ace's forehead bunched. He wagged his chin side to side. "No, no, no, son. That's not what I meant. She'll show you a whole new side of her, and you'll be rocked to the core all over again."

Chance met his father's gaze head on, something unspoken passing between them.

"I don't know what her story is," Ace continued. "Don't need to. But I see her working hard. Earning her keep. Loving this place—and, I suspect, you. That tells me plenty about her."

Chance cleared away the lump in his throat with a cough. "This talk?" He nodded, acknowledging Ace. "Means everything, Dad."

Ace rested against the cushioned back of his chair. They sat together, quietly listening to the beat of that old clock and the occasional rustle of dry oak leaves swirling around outside.

Eventually, Ace shifted in his chair and let out a harsh yawn, the back of his fist against his mouth. "That's enough sentiment for one evening," he said. "Go on. I need my rest."

The following night, the tide had just begun to retreat as all four horses made their slow descent onto the sand. Crisp and clean salt air, tinged with eucalyptus and sea spray, greeted them. Hooves left deep prints in the wet shoreline, and the sun hovered just above the horizon, casting a fiery glow over the Pacific.

Ace had given the outing his blessing this evening, waving them off from the porch where his nurse had brought him out in a wheelchair. "Ride easy," he'd said with his usual gruff smile. "And don't let Bella talk you into galloping barefoot through the surf again."

Now, Rafael and Bella were riding ahead, their horses trotting parallel to each other, their laughter floating back on the breeze.

"Tell me again why we don't do this every day?" Bella called back over her shoulder, twisting slightly in the saddle. Her dark hair fluttered beneath her hat, and she looked so utterly at home that Willow felt a flutter of FOMO, aka fear of missing out.

Bella's life held the promise of more rides like this, but all her future held was … uncertainty.

"Because some of us have to fix fences," Rafael replied to his wife, adjusting his reins. "And some of us can't afford to get sand in our boots every morning."

Bella waved him off. "Practicality is boring. Romance, sweet man. That's what this beach is for."

Chance, riding just beside Willow, chuckled under his breath.

Bella turned back toward them. "Did you know I fell in love with him right here?"

Rafael groaned good-naturedly. "Don't start."

"It's true," Bella said, undeterred. "Right there by the rocks. He let me braid wildflowers into his stirrups ..."

"She did not!" Rafael shouted into the air.

Willow smiled as the pair nudged their horses into a slow canter, heading farther up the beach, their silhouettes growing smaller against the sunlit curve of shoreline.

The sound of the surf filled the quiet as Chance slowed his gelding just slightly.

Willow sent him a questioning look.

"Just thought we could take our time."

Willow gently pulled back on her reins, too, letting her mare fall into pace beside his. The tide was low, leaving a long swath of packed sand for them to ride along. Gulls wheeled overhead, the water lapping rhythmically beside them.

They rode side-by-side for a while, silent except for the creak of leather and the occasional soft snort from the horses.

Then Chance spoke, voice low but firm. "I've been thinkin'."

"Dangerous," Willow teased gently, trying to keep it light.

He didn't smile, not right away. His jaw flexed, like he was choosing his words carefully.

"I've spent a lot of time trying to figure out where I

belong. Who I'm supposed to be. This ranch, this family … it's always been complicated."

Willow nodded, letting the rhythm of the ride keep her grounded.

"But these last few weeks …" He paused, glancing at her. "With you. Working with you. Riding with you. Watching you coax life out of a grove most folks had given up on. It's changed things."

Willow's breath caught, but she said nothing.

Chance turned in his saddle to face her more fully. His voice dropped to just above a whisper. "I don't want to go back to the way things were before you showed up."

Her pulse stuttered.

"I don't want to imagine this place—my life—without you in it."

Willow swallowed. "Chance …"

"I know you've got your past that you're worried about," he said softly. "And I've got mine, to tell you the truth. But what's happening between us is worth fighting for."

The horses slowed to a natural stop, no doubt sensing the shift in the air.

Willow took in the tautness of his shoulders, and the stillness of his grip. But there was hopefulness in his eyes too. A wanting that she had noticed before, but not fully acknowledged. Until now.

"I don't want to lose you," he whispered, his eyes scanning her face, as if waiting for a sign.

And then it came.

Her eyes filled, and he leaned in, steady and strong, and kissed her.

There was nothing rushed or reckless about it. Rather, sweet and intentional. When she'd leaned into him, his hand found the back of her neck, cupping it protectively, and his mouth discovered hers, his kiss warm and sure.

The ocean roared in the distance, even while their world narrowed to a party of two.

Willow responded before her thoughts could catch up, her hand pressing against the front of his shirt, her lips answering with all the longing she hadn't dared voice. The horses shifted slightly beneath them, but neither one moved to break the kiss.

When he pulled back, he rested his forehead lightly against hers, his breath heavy, like he'd run a race.

"You don't have to say anything," Chance murmured. "Not yet. Just … let me love you, Willow. However you need. However long it takes."

Her heart thudded like a cacophony of booming fireworks. She was out of breath. She was filled with both joy—and dread. "I don't deserve you," she whispered, picturing the simple life that was both at hand, and still terribly out of reach.

He pulled back just enough to meet her eyes, then cupped her face with his hands. "You deserve everything I can give you."

The tears she'd been holding back slipped down her cheeks in rivulets. As they sat wrapped in the hush of the evening, she let herself believe that maybe love could grow, even in uncertain soil—if only she could stop looking over her shoulder long enough to let it flourish.

Chapter 10

Willow walked the line between two older trees, adjusting the tubing she'd snaked out from the test irrigation setup that Rafael had picked up for them. A couple of ranch hands had made sure the water source was sure and open for her, but she'd asked them to leave the coiled-up tubing for her to lay out as she had planned. Every drop that reached the roots was a quiet act of restoration.

She crouched near one of the stronger saplings, testing the dampness of the soil with her fingers. Rich and dark, it held water. She smiled inwardly. A small win.

A crunch of ground pricked her ears. "Willow?"

Just the scrape of that old, familiar voice made her stomach churn. Her body stiffened, and her lungs constricted. She reached for a breath, rising slowly, dirt clinging to her hands. Her heart began to race.

The sun was behind him, making his face difficult to read at first, but that gnarled smile was unmistakable.

"Uncle Ray."

He wore crisp jeans, a tucked-in shirt that hadn't seen a

day of labor, and a belt buckle that gleamed. One hand tossed a baseball lazily into the other, the thump of leather on skin, taunting. His expression flickered between a well-practiced smile and the calculating glint of someone who'd shown up with an agenda.

"Didn't mean to spook you. Just thought I'd drop in." He glanced around. "Couldn't reach you by phone."

"You mean I hung up on you."

"Not very polite of you, niece."

"You shouldn't be here," Willow said, her voice tight. "This is private property."

"Oh, come on now." He took a step forward, spreading his arms. "It's not like I came to cause trouble. Just wanted to talk. Catch up." *Thump, thump, thump.*

She stepped back instinctively, glancing toward the barn far in the distance. No one was in sight. "We don't have anything to talk about."

"Sure we do." His voice dipped, oily again. "I'll make it simple. You've got options, Willow. A little help from you could go a long way for me. And really, what's a few thousand bucks between family?"

She felt the panic begin to rise in her chest, hot and sudden. "No."

"I'm not trying to be difficult." His eyes flicked over the grove. "It's a nice setup you've got here. Would be a shame if someone came snooping around."

Her voice rose. "You need to go, Uncle. Now!"

Gravel crunched. Boots approached. They weren't alone.

"Willow?"

Chance's voice.

Ray turned.

Willow could barely breathe. Chance walked up from behind her uncle, his eyes narrow and untrusting.

"How can I help you?" He didn't sound like he wanted to help Ray at all.

Willow opened her mouth, but her uncle spoke first.

"I'm Willow's uncle. Just dropped by to say hello and to pick something up." He swung a look at her. "Isn't that right, dear niece?"

Chance stepped between them, his stance firm, shoulders squared, eyes hard. "You're not welcome here," Chance said.

Ray raised his brows. "Easy now. No need to make a scene."

"You already did," Chance replied, voice like steel. "You come onto this land, uninvited, and start threatening her?"

Ray shrank back. He looked briefly at Willow for help. "I didn't threaten anyone."

Chance didn't budge. "You have one option: Leave and never return. Understand?"

Ray's smirk faltered. "What're you gonna do about it?"

Chance had moved so that his body completely shielded Willow's. He stayed firm, unflinching.

"First thing I'm gonna do is call my friend, Sheriff Olay." He shifted slightly. "He already has your name and description. Gave him your photo myself."

Ray's expression faltered.

"Then I'm going to stick around and watch as he cuffs you for trespassing." Chance took a step forward, leaning toward her uncle. "I'll be pressing charges by the way."

"But I'm not done talking to her ..."

"You're more than done." Chance's voice went flat. "You've worn out your welcome—and my patience."

Ray hesitated, his hand gripping that baseball so tightly

his knuckles turned white. He sent a withering stare toward Willow before turning and marching back toward the main road. Only when he was gone did Chance exhale slowly and turn toward Willow.

His eyes brushed over her face, concern tugging at the corners of his eyes. "You okay?"

She nodded, barely.

Chance's jaw worked, his forehead pulled. "You want to tell me what that was about?"

Willow crossed her arms and blew out a breath. She couldn't meet Chance's gaze. "He's been trying to get money from me. Blackmail, basically."

Chance's eyebrows lifted. "Why didn't you tell me?"

"I couldn't," she said quickly. "I was embarrassed. I didn't want anyone to know—especially not you."

"Why?"

She swallowed hard. "Because … there's one part of this whole mess I haven't told you. Something my uncle knows about."

Something in Chance's gaze flickered.

"I used some of the tainted money to buy my car. Of course, I didn't *know* it was tainted when I borrowed it …"

Chance blinked. "Wait. You mean …?" The edge in his voice lifted slightly in disbelief. "You bought *Lucille* with—?"

"With money my mom gave me," Willow said, her voice breaking. "I didn't know it was from … *that* money. Not at first. I should have asked questions, but I didn't. It felt like a gift. Like she was proud of me. I just wanted to believe it was clean."

Chance stared at her, stunned.

"I didn't mean to deceive anyone," she said. "I swear. I would've never taken that money if I'd known where it came from. By the time I found out, the car was bought and paid for. I also used a little bit to pay for school. When everything came out, when Mom got arrested and my uncle disappeared, I didn't have anything left."

She paused, waiting for a reply.

Chance shook his head once, muttering under his breath, "Lucille."

She might have smiled at the reference if his expression hadn't turned so … cold.

He turned away suddenly, running a hand down his face before letting out a frustrated breath. "I need a minute."

"Chance—"

But he was already walking away, back through the trees, his figure growing smaller as he moved toward the pasture.

Willow stood still for a long time, heart thudding painfully. Her arms crossed tightly against her chest.

She had wanted to protect this new life from all the bad news from the past. But now that the whole truth was out, and he hadn't taken it well, all she could do was watch him walk away.

TWO DAYS LATER

The kitchen never stopped.

Not for grief.

Not for guilt.

It had been forty-eight hours since they lost Ace. Forty-eight hours filled with shock, then phone calls, then neighbors dropping by with casseroles—Willow was grateful for the extra freezer in the mudroom—and nonstop chatter mixed with moments of utter silence.

Through it all, Willow kept moving. It was her job, yes, but it proved her survival too. The rhythm of the ranch kitchen had always been steady—dawn light, coffee brewing, bacon sizzling, mouths fed. Over the past day, though, Willow found herself anchored to that cadence like she was hanging onto a lifeline in a rising tide.

Hours after the news spread like fire through the ranch, Willow spotted Chance standing near his truck by the main house, head bowed, the muscles in his back and shoulders tense.

She scurried over and pulled him into a hug. "I'm so sorry, Chance."

He responded by wrapping his arms around her waist and burying his face in the crook of her neck, his embrace tight, almost desperate. But he didn't say a word, and she didn't push.

She told herself that his silence was a sign of grief. Of course, it was grief.

That still small part of her, the voice that ran outside of hers offering up counterpoints to her inner pep talks, worried about the damage she'd done to their relationship. She'd wounded him by not being completely upfront about her uncle's blackmail—and what he had on her.

And beneath the storm of silence that hung between them, she wondered if the wound she'd inflicted still stung.

So, she turned on the jets, working longer and harder. She would not let one mouth go unfed, door be unanswered, or dish stay unwashed. Running the kitchen kept her from spiraling from questions without answers.

Late afternoon sun spilled through the windows now, and for one hot second, Willow allowed herself to take in the view. It was her favorite kind of day yet felt unfair without Ace in it.

A stock pot simmered on the back burner, the aroma of chicken, celery, onion, and herbs wafting through the kitchen. Two loaves of bread cooled on a rack, and another pair browned in the oven. If ever there was a time for comfort food, this was it.

Willow moved between counters, wiping them down whether they needed it or not. She folded the same towels three times, her body running on repetition, habit, and the need to keep doing something. Anything helpful.

Eli clomped inside the kitchen, and Willow winced, picturing caked mud all over her swept floor. "Smells good, chef," he said, his voice upbeat like he was trying extra hard today. "This place smells suspiciously better than my mom's kitchen ever did."

"That's because your mom doesn't add thyme to her chicken stock." Kit bustled in behind him, carrying a covered pie dish. "By the way, I'm telling her."

Eli grabbed his heart dramatically.

Willow leaned her head to one side. "You brought pie?" She didn't mention that she'd already made two, plus three batches of cookies.

"Ace's favorite—rhubarb pie," Kit said, her faint smile flattened now. "Sorry, but I had to keep my hands busy last night, otherwise I'd have been cryin' too much."

"Oh, I understand." Willow offered her a sympathetic smile. Kit had been around the longest, since she'd dated Chance in high school. How she must've loved Ace …

Truth was, they were all in the throes of emotion right

now. She took the pie and gave Kit a one-armed hug. "Thank you. It smells delish."

Kit sniffed the air and looked around. "Wow … I think you need to sit yourself down, Willow. You've been cooking and cleaning like it's your full-time job."

"It *is* her full-time job," Eli pointed out. He lifted the soup stock lid, but Kit slapped his hand.

"Don't even think about it. That's for supper." She swung a look at Willow. "Isn't that right?"

Eli gave his wife a quick peck on the cheek, then sent a sheepish look Willow's way. The hands usually didn't end up in the kitchen like this, even the older ones like Eli, but there had been a relaxation of the rules over the past couple of days, everyone knit together over the sudden, monumental change.

"Stock's not ready yet, but you are welcome to take a sandwich from the fridge, Eli. There are plenty—in fact, take two."

"Don't have to tell me again," Eli said, opening the fridge wide. He walked away with a sandwich in each hand. "Thank you, ma'am."

Kit shook her curls and rolled her eyes.

Willow glanced to where Rafael had just entered, arms full of supply inventory. "He still giving you trouble?" Kit asked, jerking a thumb at Eli.

"He's being Eli," Rafael said, smiling as he set down the clipboard. He gave Willow a quick nod. "It's all looking good out there. We're staying ahead because you're keeping us fed."

"I just want to make sure Chance has what he needs," Willow said, adjusting a dish towel with precision. "He's got enough on his plate."

"You mean besides grief and paperwork and two dozen people asking questions he's not ready to answer?" Bella asked, stepping through the back door with an apron of her own slung casually over one shoulder.

Willow didn't respond. She didn't need to.

Bella stepped up beside her at the counter and lowered her voice. "He knows what you're doing, you know."

"I'm just helping."

"You're hiding," Bella said gently. "Feeding everyone like you're trying to earn your place. But you already have one."

Willow forced a smile. "Busy hands. Quiet mind."

"Sometimes a quiet heart matters more."

Willow focused on slicing tomatoes for the sandwich tray. "He won't really talk to me."

"That's not true," Bella said. "He talks. You both do. You're just not *saying* what matters."

Willow exhaled. "I want to. I do. But every time I look at him, I see that moment in the grove. The way he walked away. I can't tell if the silence now is grief or if he's still—"

"Wounded," Bella finished.

Willow nodded.

Bella touched her arm. "Don't be Martha right now."

Willow blinked at her.

"You're trying to serve and work your way through the ache. But maybe what's needed is what Mary chose. Sitting with the grief. Choosing presence. Even if it's uncomfortable."

Willow looked over to where Chance had been earlier in the day, at the dining table with Rafael and the ranch hands. He was gone now.

A door creaked down the hall.

Rafael walked past with the clipboard tucked under his

arm. "Chance stepped out," he said when he saw her glance around. "Didn't say where."

Bella followed her gaze. "Think he went up to the ridge?"

Willow shook her head slowly. "No. I think I know where he went."

She didn't wait for more questions. She grabbed her keys, peeled off her apron, and slipped out the back door before she could change her mind.

Outside, "Lucille" gleamed in the afternoon light, as if proud of who she was, despite her misbegotten origins. Willow slid behind the wheel and turned the key, the engine rumbling to life with a sputter and a cough.

"Come on, girl," she murmured, coaxing the tiny box of a car to life.

The road stretched out in front of her, winding west through the ranch gate, past the rows of olive trees that had come to symbolize her second chance—and her greatest mistake.

She didn't know what she'd say when she found him.

Didn't know if she'd cry or apologize or just sit beside him and let the ocean do the talking.

But she knew one thing for sure.

She wasn't going to let him carry this grief alone. Not anymore.

She pressed her foot to the gas, and Lucille sped toward the beach.

Toward him.

Toward whatever came next.

The beach was nearly empty.

Low tide left a long mirror of damp sand between the shore and the slow-rolling waves. Overhead, gulls called to one another like sentinels. The sun had begun its descent to the horizon, and though it was still early, the sky showed promise of a spectacular show to come.

Willow pulled Lucille into the same turnout they'd parked in days ago—the same windswept edge where Bella had declared her love story, and where Chance had kissed her like he meant forever.

Her boots crunched softly on the ground as she made her way down the sloped trail. Salty air landed on her tongue, and she licked her lips, the memory of him not far away.

When she reached the sand, she slipped out of her boots, digging toes in deep. When she straightened, she spotted him.

Chance stood at the water's edge, back to her, arms folded as he stared out at the surf. He hadn't changed out of his work shirt—rolled-up sleeves, jeans still clinging to his hips—and yet he looked like he belonged.

Willow hesitated. Her chest ached for his unimaginable loss.

She didn't know how to bridge the space between them. Not after what she'd hidden. Not after he'd walked away only to lose his father hours later.

But she took a breath and stepped forward anyway.

He didn't turn when she approached, but his voice resonated low and steady. "Figured you'd come."

She stopped beside him, close enough to feel the heat from his body. "I wasn't sure I should."

Silence. Then, "You should."

More quiet passed between them, waves rushing forward and retreating again.

"I'm sorry. About everything. About not telling you sooner. About trying to carry it alone."

Chance finally turned to look at her. His eyes, blue gray like a storm held just beneath the surface, met hers.

"I hate that my secret hurt you," Willow went on, her throat tightening. "I didn't know how to tell you about my uncle's demands. I felt so ashamed. About the car, the money … what it meant. I didn't want to bring that mess into your world."

"You didn't bring in a mess," Chance said softly. "You brought yourself."

She blinked.

"And I want *all* of you," he continued. "Not just the good parts. Not just the pretty story."

He closed the space between them, his voice gentler than the waves. "What happened with your family, with Lucille— that doesn't change a thing for me."

Willow shook her head slightly. "How can it not?"

"Because I love you," Chance said, firm and certain. "No matter what."

Her breath caught.

"But if we're gonna do this—really do this—you've gotta trust me. With everything." His eyes searched hers. "Even the parts that scare you. Even the things you'd rather bury. That's the only way this works."

Willow looked down, her voice small. "I'm not used to

that. People haven't always stuck around when they learned the full story."

"I'm not people," he said.

She looked up again, and he reached for her hand, gentle, but sure.

"I know grief," he said. "I know guilt. I know what it's like to carry something around so long it feels like part of you."

He paused, then added, "But I also know what it means to lay it down. To let someone else help carry it."

Willow blinked fast, a tear slipping free despite her best efforts.

"I was trying so hard to protect this life I've built," she whispered. "To protect *you*. And, in the process, I hurt the one person I was trying to keep."

Chance brushed the tear away with his thumb. "I don't need protecting, Willow. I need honesty. I need *you*."

She leaned into his hand, unable to pull away. "I don't want to lose you," she whispered.

"Then don't."

He tugged her forward until she was against his chest, his arms wrapped around her. Her hands slipped around his waist, holding on, no thought of letting go.

The tide brushed ever closer, and the sun slipped lower, streaking the water in gold. Neither of them spoke—there was no need. The words had already done their work.

Eventually, Chance leaned back just enough to catch her eyes. "One question, though."

Willow arched a brow. "Only one?"

He gave a slow grin. "Why exactly did you decide to spend hush money on the world's ugliest car?"

Willow laughed, the sound catching in her throat. "Hey now—*you* named her Lucille, remember?"

"I did," he admitted. "Seemed only right for a salmon-colored shoebox with the attitude of a rodeo bull."

"She's reliable," Willow said, chin lifting.

"She's a cautionary tale," he shot back. "But I'll give her this—she got you here."

Their eyes met again, and lightness settled over them. They held hands, the ocean whispering behind them, the tension that once held them tight now unraveled into something steadier. Truer.

"Come back with me," Chance said after a while, voice deep.

"I never left."

He nodded once, like he believed her now. Then he glanced up the hill to where his truck sat waiting. For a beat, he didn't move.

"Don't feel like being alone just yet," he said.

"Then don't be."

He quirked a smile at her. "You want me to ride up the hill in that rickety car of yours?"

"I dare you. One of the guys can get your car later."

"Fine." He stretched an arm around her. "I'll ride shotgun. But I swear, if that car makes another sound like a dying cow, I'm walking."

Willow smiled, wide and unguarded for the first time in a long, long while. "Deal."

"Something's different." Bella peered at Willow with inquisitive eyes. "You're glowing."

"So anyway," Willow was saying, holding up a fresh jar of Topa Gold in the sunlight, "I think this is our best batch yet. It's a good thing we took a closer look at those trees over in the eastern corner. Still had some good juice on them."

Bella squinted down the hill. "And why were Joey and Luke driving Chance's truck into the compound yesterday? I saw them real early. He never lets anyone drive his truck."

Willow set a second jar of oil into the basket. "Pretty sure this is good enough to be tossed onto pasta with some fresh garlic. Maybe add some grated parm on top too."

Bella poked a fist into her side. "What aren't you telling me?"

Willow sent a sly smile Bella's way.

"Oh my gosh, you and Chance … you're *finally* a couple!" She turned her chin and pointed a finger. "Tell me I'm right."

"For heaven's sake, can't a girl have any secrets from you?" Willow tsked.

"No, they cannot!" Bella threw her arms around Willow. "I'm so happy for you two. It was so obvious how *perfect* you were for each other."

Willow laughed, squeezed her back, and let the news wash over her for the millionth time. Chance loved her. She loved him back. Everything was good for a change.

Well, almost everything …

Willow swung a look across the grove where Chance and Rafael worked together to move a fence line marking a new boundary for grazing. She pushed fearful thoughts from her mind, and focused on the good.

Gratefulness washed over her at witnessing Chance and

Rafael's partnership, especially after the tension of the fore-man's first couple of weeks on the ranch.

In the days since Ace's passing, Chance had taken up the mantle his father left behind. He'd taken on extraordinary responsibilities with grace, grit, and even some moments of humor.

Like continuing the ribbing about poor old Lucille. He moaned and groaned the whole way home from the beach, like he'd bruised every part of that handsome body of his along the ride.

As if.

Even the ranch hands got in on it and started teasing her about her poor car:

Does that thing run on gas or broken promises?

That car's the reason the chickens won't cross the road.

And the one that had Bella giggling for five minutes straight: *It's so optimistic … like it thinks it's really a car!*

She was laughing in spite of herself when Chance looked up from his work, tipped his hat back and sent a grin her way.

Willow smiled back, gave Bella a quick hug, then made her way toward Chance, the basket bumping against her hip.

"Hey."

"Hey, yourself."

He took off his hat and kissed her tenderly.

Rafael snickered.

Chance cut a look at the foreman. "Don't you have some cow patties to round up?"

Rafael chuckled. He dusted his hands off, saying, "I know when I'm not wanted."

"No offense," Willow said.

Rafael smiled. "None taken." He clapped Chance on the shoulder. "I'm going to walk the southern ridge before supper. Holler if you need anything."

Chance nodded. "Tell Bella to save us some of those lemon bars."

Rafael gave a mock salute and disappeared between the rows.

Willow put the basket on the ground. "You've settled in nicely to all this." She paused, placing her hands near his shoulders. "How are you really doing?"

Chance's expression softened. "Still feels strange sometimes. Walking into that office and knowing Ace isn't there. Making decisions without even a nod from him."

"He knew you could handle it. That's why he did what he did."

Chance wrapped his arms tighter about her waist, and buried his face in her hair, sighing. "Hope so."

She pulled back slightly, looking into his eyes. "Nuh-uh. Not hope so, *know* so."

"Ace was right about you."

"Right? About what?"

He grinned. "You're good for me. He said as much."

Willow pouted and put one hand on her heart. "He said that? That's so sweet, but I-I haven't done much."

"Are you kidding me? You've done everything." His voice was quiet now, steady. "You've held the kitchen, this house, this whole place together while I found my footing—even before Dad's passing. And you did it while carrying your own grief. Your own story."

She looked away for a moment, blinking back the sudden warmth in her eyes.

He reached for her hand. "I've been thinking."

"Oh, now, haven't I told you that's dangerous?" She echoed the same words she'd said on the beach.

Chance grinned, his gaze growing serious.

"I was kidding, you know."

"The thing is, I'm not." His brows shifted, like he had a secret. He pulled something from his pocket and held it inside his palm.

Willow frowned.

He opened his palm. There lay a ring—simple, elegant, set with a pale green sapphire that shimmered and sparkled like silvery leaves from one of her beloved olive trees.

Willow froze, her breath catching somewhere in her chest.

"Let's not waste another minute," Chance said. "Marry me?"

She gasped.

"I want a life with you, Willow. Not someday. Not down the line. *Now*. Here. At this place we're working to hold onto. In this grove, where everything started."

Willow's voice came out in a whisper. "Are you sure?"

"Never been more sure of anything," he said, holding the ring up for her to take. "Say yes, and we'll build something that lasts. Something rooted and real."

Willow looked at the ring, then at him, her heart both melting and roaring in her chest. The smile on her face could not have been wider. She held out her ring finger. He gave her a questioning look, and she nodded.

She may have even squealed a little as he slid the exquisite ring onto her finger.

Chance let out a long, slow breath, as if he'd been holding

it until she said yes. He pulled her into his arms, smiling like the sun had just risen again.

Willow laughed and buried her face against his chest, nothing but love … and trust … for this man.

For a long while, they stood in the meadow, listening to wind rustle the grasses around them and whip through the nearby grove of olives.

After a time, Chance pulled back and peered down at here. "There's something else."

Willow leaned her head to the side, waiting.

"I've been thinking about your mom."

Willow's smile faltered. "Yes." She sighed.

"Listen to me." He held her gaze. "You said she'll be fully released soon, right? That she'll need care, supervision, stability."

She nodded quickly, a tinge of sadness eclipsing her happiness. Of course, she wanted her mother to be released —her sentence had been so harsh. But she'd yet to figure out where the best place for her would be.

He continued. "I know she's made mistakes. We all have. But I also know what it feels like to carry something too heavy on your own."

Willow blinked,

"Bring her here. To the ranch."

Her hand flew to her mouth, dawn opening up in her mind. "Chance, I can't ask that of you."

"You're not asking. I'm offering. She can move into your cottage, and you'll move in with me." A small smile lit his face. "We'll get her some care, Hopefully, this place can help heal more than just us."

Tears flowed, slipping down her cheeks. How much more

joy could she take? Willow could barely find the words. "Y-you amaze me."

He kissed her forehead, then her cheek, then whispered against her temple. "I love you, Willow."

"Love you back, cowboy."

Then they swayed together beneath the cool wind, growing more intertwined with each passing moment.

Epilogue

Willow stood just beyond view, tucked behind a makeshift screen made from trellises and vines, the olive trees rustling in the distance like a chorus of angels. She had come to this ranch all those months ago, hoping for a paycheck and a safe place to lay her head at night, if only for a while. But what she found encompassed so much more—love, a home, and a future filled with promises and hope.

Her dress was simple—ivory lace, vintage-cut, and embellished with tulle. A dream. She carried a bouquet of wildflowers, bright flecks of yellow, white, and green, that trembled slightly in her hands. Maybe from nerves. Mostly from awe.

Her mother sat on the aisle, her silver hair swept up and held with an abalone-shell clip. A light cardigan hung across her shoulders despite the warmth. Her caregiver, a kind woman named Marisol, sat beside her, chatting with other guests. Ruthie looked steady, present, and happy. She turned a look over her shoulder and waved her handkerchief at Willow, her smile big, proud.

When Willow had asked her mother if she wanted to live on the ranch, Ruthie had said yes with a kind of astonishment, as if she still didn't fully believe she'd been given a second chance.

Neither did Willow, some days.

"You ready?" Bella appeared beside her, beaming and beautiful in a dusty blue dress that matched the sky. "Because I am not emotionally prepared to watch you walk down that aisle looking like a poem."

Willow laughed, her eyes stinging. "You're ridiculous."

"And you're stunning." Bella looped her arm through Willow's. "Kit's got tissues. Rafael's already cried twice, and your groom keeps pacing by the arbor like he's trying not to bolt—which, let's be honest, is on brand."

Willow peeked around the corner. Chance stood in front of the arbor, talking quietly with his two brothers. It was still strange seeing them all in one place—Caleb in his crisp fire dress blues, and Micah in a rumpled blazer and tortoiseshell glasses. One smelled faintly of smoke, the other of book pages and coffee.

They had flown in months earlier for Ace's memorial but hadn't lingered long. Grief had scattered them like leaves in a hard wind. This time, they'd flown in early, had spent time on the old ranch, observing the changes. Mainly, though, they'd come back to stand beside their brother.

Micah clapped Chance on the back and said something that made him laugh—a deep, real laugh that traveled all the way to where Willow stood.

Her heart caught.

"I'm ready," she whispered.

Bella gave her a swift kiss on the cheek. "I'll say you are." She stepped down the aisle and took her place at the front. The music started—guitar and fiddle, light and lilting—and Willow stepped onto the rose-strewn path.

She barely noticed the crowd, though familiar faces filled every row. Ranch hands in pressed shirts and cleaned-up boots. Neighbors, friends. Rafael beaming at the front, blinking hard with a grin bigger than she'd ever seen.

But all Willow saw was Chance.

He stood straighter when he saw her, his eyes bright and wide and just a little stunned. He didn't fidget now. He didn't pace. He just waited.

And when she reached him, he took her hands in his, steady and warm, and the rest of the world went quiet.

The ceremony was short and heartfelt, with words from the heart and scripture to seal their vows. Rafael, officiating with a tie slightly crooked and a prayer card in his front pocket, spoke of love that digs deep and chooses again every morning. He spoke of roots. Of olive trees. Of Ace.

"We miss him today," Rafael said, voice low but clear. "But he's here. In the land. In the legacy. In the strength of the man Chance has become."

Chance's eyes glistened. Willow squeezed his hand.

Micah stepped forward to read a blessing. Caleb followed with a few quiet words about family, service, and how his little brother somehow ended up in charge of more than just livestock.

And then, they spoke their vows.

"I don't want just the parts you think are safe to give," Chance said, "I want all of you. Every truth, every joy, every scar."

Willow's voice trembled when she answered. "You never

asked me to be anything I'm not. And I've never felt safer than I do with you."

After the rings were exchanged, Rafael said, "By the power vested in me by the State of California—and because Bella said I had to—I now pronounce you husband and wife."

Cheers rose like thunder. Willow barely heard them.

Chance pulled her close, kissed her in that slow, reverent way that said home wasn't a place—it was a person. And he'd found his.

Later, as the sun began to set, Willow stood beneath the largest olive tree, watching lanterns glow to life across the hill. They'd set up outside, where the warm weather made lingering easy and doable.

Tables were being cleared. Someone had started music again, low and sweet.

Her mother sat with Marisol under a wide umbrella, chatting softly with Bella. Every now and then, Ruthie's gaze would drift to Willow, and she'd smile that quiet, wistful smile again.

"I didn't know joy could be this quiet," Chance said, stepping up behind her, arms sliding around her waist.

She leaned back into him, her eyes lolling. "I didn't know joy could be felt this deeply."

He pressed his lips to her temple. "I booked the honeymoon."

She turned slightly in surprise. "You did?"

"Two weeks. Coastal cabin. No cell signal. Just water and rest and you."

Willow grinned. "You spoil me, my saltwater cowboy."

"I plan to make a habit of it."

She turned fully to face him. "Think the ranch will survive without us?"

He glanced back toward the trees, where fairy lights twinkled between branches like stars come early. "It will. It's got strong roots."

Willow slipped her hand into his. "So do we."

And just like that, the past slipped away, the present settled into promise, and the future stretched ahead—wide and wild and waiting.

Ah, wasn't that a sweet and romantic story? Want to know more about how Rafael and Bella met and fell in love? (It's a reader favorite!) Make sure to pick up Beach Music, where a bachelor auction and a winning bid catch Bella—and Rafael— by surprise.

Acknowledgments

Thank you for reading *Her Saltwater Cowboy*. This story grew from a few sparks of curiosity after I finished writing *Beach Music*. I kept wondering what life on the Sutter Creek Ranch looked like—and now we know! I'm so grateful you chose to come along for the ride.

Huge thanks to my family—Dan, Matt, Angie, Emma, and my mom, Elaine F. Navarro—for their constant encouragement and for listening to me ramble through plot twists and deadlines. And a tail-wag of thanks to my loyal writing companion, Dancer.

I'm also grateful to my editor, Dione Benson, for her thoughtful guidance throughout the editing of this project.

Most of all, thank you, dear reader, for spending time in the pages of this story. If you enjoyed *Her Saltwater Cowboy*, I'd be honored if you'd leave a review or share it with a friend.

With gratitude,
Julie

<u>**Otter Bay Novels**</u>

Sweet Waters (book 1)

A Shore Thing (book 2)

Fade to Blue (book 3)

<u>The Chocolate Series</u>

Chocolate Beach (book 1)

Truffles by the Sea (book 2)

Mocha Sunrise (book 3)

<u>Cottage Grove Cozy Mysteries</u>

The Christmas Thief (book 1)

The Christmas Killer (book 2)

The Christmas Heist (book 3)

Cottage Grove Mysteries (books 1-3)

About the Author

JULIE CAROBINI is the author dozens of inspirational beach romances. Her books feature captivating heroines, endearing heroes, and a cast of quirky friends, all bound together by the secrets they keep. Her bestselling titles include *Walking on Sea Glass, Runaway Tide,* and *Reunion in Saltwater Beach*. Julie has received awards for writing and editing from The National League of American Pen Women and ACFW, and she is a double finalist for the ACFW Carol Award. She is the mother of three grown kids and lives on the California coast with her husband, Dan, and their rescue pup, Dancer.

Please visit her at
www.juliecarobini.com

www.ingramcontent.com/pod-product-compliance
Lightning Source LLC
Chambersburg PA
CBHW032305310726
48973CB00008B/2529